The Black Flamingo

The Black Flamingo

DEAN ATTA

hodder

HODDER CHILDREN'S BOOKS

First published in Great Britain in 2019 by Hodder and Stoughton

1 3 5 7 9 10 8 6 4 2

Printed and bound in Great Britain by Clays Ltd, Elcograf S.p.A.

The paper and board used in this book are made
from wood from responsible sources.

Hodder Children's Books
An imprint of
Hachette Children's Group
Part of Hodder and Stoughton
Carmelite House
50 Victoria Embankment
London EC4Y 0DZ

An Hachette UK Company
www.hachette.co.uk
www.hachettechildrens.co.uk

for George

PROLOGUE

I am the black flamingo.
The black flamingo is me
trying to find myself.
This book is a fairy tale
in which I am the prince
and the princess. I am
the king and the queen.
I am my own wicked
witch and fairy godmother.

This book is a fairy tale
in which I'm cursed
and blessed by others.

But, finally, I am the fairy
finding my own magic.

When female
flamingos lay eggs in
the zoo, the eggs are taken
from them and put into incubators.
The zoo keepers give dummy eggs
to flamingo couples to nest with, while
the zookeepers watch their behaviour
to figure out who will make the best
flamingo parents. When the incubated
eggs are almost ready to hatch they
decide which couple will be given
normal eggs and which will be
left with those that never
contained precious life.

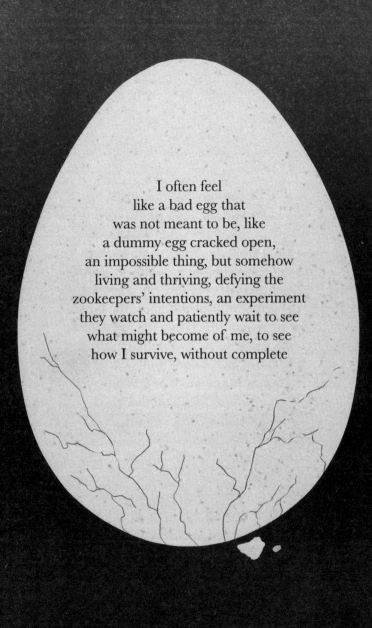

I often feel
like a bad egg that
was not meant to be, like
a dummy egg cracked open,
an impossible thing, but somehow
living and thriving, defying the
zookeepers' intentions, an experiment
they watch and patiently wait to see
what might become of me, to see
how I survive, without complete

love.

I was born in London,
two months before the end of the world,
on 31st October 1999.

Mummy tells me,
'When we got closer to the millennium,
people thought planes would fall from the sky
and clocks in computers would go back
one hundred years. But time cannot go back.
We can only move forward.'

I am a baby, just hatched.
My only feathers are my tiny eyelashes.

Over my gurgling, I don't hear my father
telling Mummy, 'I'm too young to be a dad.'

Mummy tells me all this, when I'm old enough.

How six days before the millennium,
she burnt their Christmas dinner
and he shouted, 'You're useless!'
before throwing his plate down, turkey
stuck to the kitchen floor, and I cried,
startled by early indoor fireworks.

That was the end for them. The beginning
for Mummy and me.

BARBIES AND BELONGING

Today is my sixth birthday
and I'm hiding in my room.

Last year, for my birthday,
Uncle B bought me this
Casio watch. *Look* – it lights up
and is water-resistant. That means
I can wear it in the bath.

Last night, when Mummy was
making dinner, I snuck into
her bedroom and looked inside
her wardrobe, parting clothes
to see the back where she
always hides my presents.

I picked up the parcel, feeling
the shape of the long, thin box,
inside the silver wrapping paper.

It was definitely the right shape
to be

a Barbie!

I carefully peeled
the Sellotape at one end
and peeked underneath
the wrapping paper
at the top of the box,
to see a green logo:

Teenage Mutant Ninja Turtles.

I told Mummy two months ago,
'If you only get me one present
this year, *please* can it be

a Barbie?'

'Michael Brown,'
calls Mummy, 'where are you?
Come down and open your birthday present.
Your friends will be arriving soon!'

I stand at the top of our stairs
and shout down,
'Is it a Barbie?'

Mummy comes to the bottom step,
smiling gently.
'No, Michael, I didn't think you were
serious. But I got you something
that I know you'll love.'

I watch a tear
land on the wooden floor
between my Turtles slippers –

a gift from Aunty B last Christmas.

Mummy comes upstairs, embracing me
in a soft, warm, Mum-smelling hug.
'Oh, darling, I can get you a Barbie
for Christmas, if you still want one.'

Christmas is ages away.

I'm about to cry again when the doorbell rings.

Emily, Amber, Laura, Toby and Jamal
have all come round for birthday tea
with their mums.

Callum is the last one to arrive.
His dad brings him but doesn't stay
like the mums do.

Callum and Emily don't like each other.

Callum lives in a flat with his dad.
They play video games together
and eat takeaways for dinner
and sometimes Callum gets to stay up
and watch TV all night, if his dad is out;
it must be so much fun.

Callum is mixed the same
way as me, a black dad and white mummy,
but he doesn't live with his mummy
and I don't live with my dad.

Mummy has made stuffed vine leaves,
stuffed peppers and Greek salad.
There's olives, carrot sticks, pitta bread
and hummus, which I love, and taramasalata,
which I think tastes yucky but I love the word.

I teach my friends how to pronounce it:
Ta-ra-ma-sa-la-ta. Tarama-salata.

'What is it?' asks Callum. 'And why is it pink?'

'It's fish eggs,' I say, proudly, 'and my mummy
told me it's dyed pink. I think it looks pretty.'

'But it tastes disgusting!' Callum says,
spitting it back out onto his plate. 'I *hate* pink.'
He scowls, looking straight at Emily.

Later, I blow out six candles
on my Teenage Mutant Ninja Turtles birthday
cake and make
my wish
for

a Barbie.

Emily's playroom is a bubble-gum-
pink mess. She has 42 Barbies;
I know because I counted. She also has
four ponies and six Jeeps for them.
Goddess of Beauty looks brand new.

When Emily shows her to me
she says, 'She's meant to be
the Greek goddess, Aphrodite,
but she looks like your mummy.'

Emily has lots of toys but this doll
captivates me, her flowing white
and blue gown and her gold headband.

I pick up some of her other Barbies
with their missing arms, legs, heads.
'Why don't they have full bodies?'

'Their heads came off when I was brushing
their hair,' Emily says, but I've never seen
Emily use a Barbie hairbrush. The one
for Goddess is still in its packet. I take it out
and gently brush her hair.

'I'm going to ask my mummy to get me
this one for Christmas,' I tell Emily, proudly.

Christmas morning,
I race downstairs to find
a present under the tree.

No wrapping paper, just
a pink bow on the box.
Mummy has bought me

a Barbie!

But she got it wrong.
It's not the Goddess
but I hug her anyway.
'Thank you, Mummy.'

This Barbie doesn't have long, dark, curly hair
or dark eyes like Mummy's,
like the Goddess.

I decide to name my doll Phoebe.

Phoebe looks like Emily.

I don't cut Phoebe's long, blonde hair
or pull off her head or any of her limbs
like Emily would.

Phoebe is not
the Barbie I wanted
but she's the Barbie I've got,
and I decide to take care of her.

Uncle B arrives in his black BMW
to pick me up to take me to Granny B's
for Christmas dinner with my dad
and the rest of the Brown family.

As I leave, Mummy grabs my shoulders
and turns me around, smiles
and puts out her hand. 'Michael, please
can you leave Phoebe here?
I need her to help me clean up.'

It's only a ten-minute drive in Uncle's BMW
but it feels alien.
I wish Mummy was coming with us.

I'm happy when we arrive, because the family
cheer and I think it must be for me.
Aunty B yells, 'Finally, we can eat!'

'First, we muss pray,' says Granny B.
Everyone bows their head.
'Faada God, we tank you dat Mikey
can be wid us dis special day, we pray
dat he is neva a stranger to you or to
dis family. In Jesus's name, amen.'

Everyone at the table repeats, 'Amen.'

My dad comes down from his bedroom.

There is a spare seat and place laid out for him
next to me. He silently piles his food up and
takes his plate back upstairs.

'Hey, Mikey – that's great!' Uncle B says,
looking around the table at everyone else.
'That's two Christmas crackers we can pull
together!'

Boxing Day.
Emily and I are playing
in my room.

She's brought Goddess Barbie with her,
who has a shaved head now.

Emily sees Phoebe and asks,
'Couldn't your mummy afford
the one you wanted?'

I feel myself getting hot.
I reach under my bed for my
black Action Man toy from Uncle B,
kept in his box, which he says is vintage.

On the front is Action Man's name,
'TOM STONE', and in his picture,
holding a big gun, he wears a green hat
and camouflage outfit.

I proudly say, 'Look what my uncle got me.
Shall we get him out?'
Emily closes her eyes to make him disappear
and says, 'He looks scary.'

A few days later, we're in Emily's playroom.
Emily pulls out a brand new Barbie from her
fairy backpack.
Versace Barbie.

'Versace is a fashion designer,' Emily says.
'Mummy has two dresses by Versace. Daddy
bought them for her.' She pauses. 'Michael,
do you have a daddy, too?'

'No, my mummy buys her *own* dresses.'

For my seventh birthday, instead of
another Barbie, I tell Mummy I want to change
my last name. I tell her I want to match her.
I want to change my surname from
his Brown to her Angeli.

Mum once told me, 'Angeli means "angel"
or "messenger".'

She kneels down and puts her hands
on my shoulders, asks, 'Are you sure?
You're very young to make these kinds
of decisions. What about Granny Brown
and Aunty Brown and Uncle Brown?
They all do such nice things for you.'

I reply, 'They do, but you do the most
nice things.'

She smiles and hugs me tightly.

I hug her back; I count ten seconds
in my head and then drop my arms
to my side but Mummy doesn't let go for
another nine seconds. Nineteen seconds
is the longest hug I have ever had.

On my seventh birthday, after my presents,
Mummy hands me a piece of paper:
'Change of Name Deed, Michael Angeli'.

But I read: 'Name Dead'
and it makes sense.

I don't want *his* name
dragging behind me like a dead dog on a lead,

like toilet roll on the sole
of my new Kickers boots,

like a shedded snakeskin,

like a second shadow,

like the thick vapour trails
of the Red Arrows,
diesel mixed with coloured dye,

making a mark in the sky.
I don't need a plane because
with my new name I can really fly.

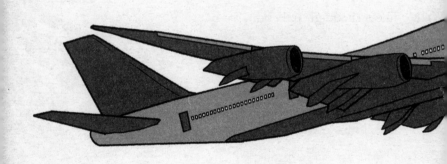

That night
I have a dream
in which Mummy is killed
when a British Airways Boeing 747
crashes into our house.
The left wing cuts through her
bedroom window but I survive.

Would I live with my Uncle B,
Aunty B or Granny B?
Or would I become an orphan?

Mum's gone out and her new boyfriend,
Trevor, lets me watch a horror movie
called *Nightmare on Elm Street*.

I am fascinated by the man
in the red and green striped jumper
who visits people in their dreams
and kills them. At school I describe
what he does and the glove he wears.
Knives for fingers. I swipe at the air
and children run away screaming,
except Callum, who just laughs and then
says, 'Go on, then, rip my guts out!'
Smiling and holding open his navy blue blazer.

The next day, the head teacher calls
Mum after complaints from the other parents.

'Children are having nightmares,'
she tells me when she sends me to bed
early, but I sit at the top of the stairs.

'What were you thinking?' Mum shouts
at Trevor. 'He's only seven years old.'

Trevor speaks quietly and I can't make out his reply.

'You really don't think you've done
anything wrong, do you?' Mum laughs.
'He's not your son. It's not for you
to decide what he's old enough for.'

'So why did you leave him with me?' Trevor shouts.

'Because you said you wanted to
bond with him. I didn't think you meant
by showing him Freddy-effing-Krueger.'

I hate hearing her shout.
It makes my tummy feel funny.
But mostly I feel bad
for getting Trevor into trouble.

I am eight
when my sister,
Anna,
is placed
into the nest of her
white-wicker Moses basket,
newly hatched,
a chick
for me to help
Mum
raise
for the whole of the summer holiday.

Crying
for her thumb to suck
when I tuck her hands
under her
tiny torso.

Anna is a living doll.
A brown-skinned Barbie.
Mum lets me pick out
her outfit each morning.

When
school starts again,
I count down the hours
until
I can run
home and see Anna.

My favourite thing
is to sing to Anna:

'Itsy Bitsy Spider',
'Baa, Baa, Black Sheep',
'Twinkle, Twinkle, Little Star'
and other nursery rhymes.

Mum asks if I want
to have singing lessons.

Trevor takes me
in his cool silver Audi
every Saturday morning.

Anna has a different dad
but we have the same surname.

Mum decided
and Trevor didn't argue.

In the dining hall at school,
I explain to Callum: 'Trevor is Anna's dad
but not mine.'

Callum asks, 'If you have different dads,
isn't she your *half*-sister?'

When I get home,
I ask, 'Mummy, are we only half?'

'Don't let anyone tell you
that you are **half** anything.
You and Anna are
simply brother and sister.

Don't let anyone tell you
that she's your **half-sister**.

Don't let anyone tell you
that you are **half-black**
and **half-white**. **Half-Cypriot**
and **half-Jamaican**.

You are a full human
being. It's never as simple
as being half and half.

You are born in Britain.
You need to make space
for what British means.

What it means to you
to be British, Cypriot
and Jamaican, too; but
it's only for you to decide.'

SANDCASTLES

At school, we play Kiss Chase.

When we were in the little playground we had
toys to play with but here in the big playground
we just have each other.

I usually chase Amber and Laura,
who slow down when I chase them,
and speed up when Callum runs after them,
but he always catches up, eventually.

Emily shakes her head at Callum
and says 'Time out' when he runs towards her.
Emily and I have agreed not to kiss.
'Because best friends don't kiss,' says Emily.
I don't mind not kissing Emily.

I don't tell Emily that
when no one else can see, behind the big tree,
I kiss Callum and Jamal and Toby.

Once a week, Mum lets me have
one friend over for dinner after school.
This week I've invited Callum.
Whilst Mum is cooking, we play husband
and wife, in my bedroom.

I play the wife. In an imaginary kitchen
I cook and Callum pretends
to return from work, hugs me from behind
and kisses me on the cheek.

I say, 'Dinner's ready!'
Serve his imaginary meal, tell him
what it is, so he knows how to enjoy it:
'It's spaghetti,' I say. 'You've got to use
the spoon and fork.'

Callum asks, 'Why can't we have pizza
like the Turtles?' Pointing to the poster
on my wall.

'Because we're not playing Turtles now,' I say.
'How was your day at work, darling?'

I script and direct this role-play game,
I play it with Toby and Jamal, too.
Just not with Emily, Amber or Laura.

All the girls in my class like me.
I'm the only boy invited to their sleepovers.
'Michael, are you free Friday night?'
'Michael, do you like Disney and ice cream?'

I share blankets on the floor with four,
five, six girls or more.

Emily is always invited because
she's the most popular girl in our class.

Callum says, 'You're so lucky!'

These girls are my friends.
I do feel lucky.

'When is Trevor coming back?'
I eventually stop asking Mum.

She takes me
to my singing lessons now.

Trevor returns
in his stupid silver car,
demanding
to see Anna.

But he never asks to see me.

The night I realise
Trevor isn't coming back,
I have the dream
in which mum is killed
when a Boeing 747
crashes into our house.
The left wing cuts through her
bedroom window but Anna and I survive.

Would Trevor take Anna
but leave me an orphan?

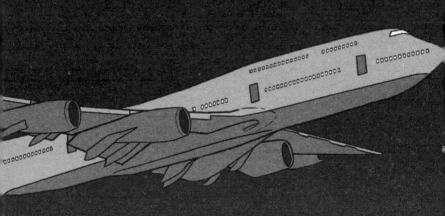

Anna gets Phoebe, my old Barbie doll,
and my Teenage Mutant Ninja Turtles.
Anna gets my dungarees
and all my other old clothes, too.
I notice when Anna plays
with my Turtles, no one asks her why.
I notice when Anna wears
my dungarees, no one comments.
I'm glad she is free to play
and dress however she feels happy.

Mum takes me and Anna to Brighton Beach.
Anna brings my yellow bucket and spade,
which she insists on holding for the whole
train journey. I already know – and Mum
explained – that the beach has pebbles and
rocks, not sand.

Walking from the station towards the beach,
I dread Anna's disappointment
but when we get there she takes my hand
and lets go of Mum.
'Stay where I can see you two,' Mum shouts
after us, as Anna leads me to the water's edge.

She kneels down and piles pebbles in
the bucket. 'Sandcastle,' she says, beaming.
'Sandcastle.'

I sit on the bench under the tree
playing Cat's Cradle with Emily,
when Laura and Amber come over.

'Michael!' 'Please sing!'
'Come on, Michael.' 'Pretty please, sing us
a pop song!'

'I don't want to be a show-off,' I protest.
I prefer musicals anyway.

'Of course you do,' says Emily.
'Why else do you have singing lessons?'

There is one pop song I love
right now: 'Lady Marmalade'.
I sing the verses by Christina Aguilera,
Mýa and Pink, and Lil' Kim's rap.

A big group of girls, and some boys,
gather around, some giggle but most cheer.

I hear a wolf-whistle and I think
it comes from either Jamal or Toby.

I direct the song to Callum, who is at the back
of the crowd. When I point at him, they all
turn around. He shakes his head. Walks away.

The bell rings and everyone starts heading
into school. Emily grabs my navy blue blazer.

I turn back to face her. 'What's up?'

She looks down at her Kickers, then back up.
'Do you know what the French words mean?'
she asks.

I shake my head. She whispers
in my ear, a new truth. I never knew it was
about more than kissing.

It's non-uniform day.
Mum has picked out a brand new Levi's denim
jacket. It's stiff and uncomfortable.

I take it off at the start of the day, hang it
on my cloakroom hook.
When I go back
before home time, it's gone.

At the school gate I say, 'Mummy,
I think someone took my jacket by mistake.'

She shouts, 'What do you mean
someone took it? You stupid boy,
you have to look after your things!
Do you know how much it cost?'

'I didn't like it anyway,' I say, embarrassed
that people might be watching.

She slaps me hard across the face.

My eyes fill up but I don't blink.
I look her straight in the eye,
'You're not allowed to do that.'

'Uncle B, Mum hit me.
I think she's worried about money.'

Uncle B has always been there for me.
The only person in the Brown family
that I see regularly.

He tells me that Mum is doing her best.
He tells me how hard he worked
to build himself a better life,
get the family out of poverty.

He buys me gifts
but this is not why I love him.
He likes planes and astronomy;
he has his head in the clouds,
reaches for stars.

MUSIC AND STARS

I'm singing 'Twinkle, Twinkle,
Little Star' with Anna,
helping Mum to put her to bed.

Mum says, 'You have such a beautiful voice,
Michael, your singing teacher told me
about a special school
you could go to with an excellent choir.
It's an all-boys school in Camden.'

I like boys. I like Camden.
I like when we go to Camden Market.
It's full of crazy, colourful clothes.
We walk by the canal after,
if it's a sunny day. But we don't go often
because it's far away.

Emily is going to a private school
that Mum says we can't afford.

Callum says he doesn't know
what school he's going to yet.
But Callum doesn't sing,
so he can't come with me.

I have to audition to get in
because we don't live
in the catchment area.
We have to take the Tube
and then the Overground to get there.

The bald man playing piano
is Mr Evans, and the blonde
woman watching me is Mrs Evans.

I sing, 'Where Is Love?'
from the musical *Oliver!*
Even though Oliver sings
this song about his mum,
I sing about my dad instead.
I change 'she' to 'he'.

Mr and Mrs Evans both cry
while I sing.
I get in.

To celebrate,
Uncle B takes me
to Farnborough Airshow
to see the Red Arrows.

I love their speed and grace,
red, white and blue vapour trails
behind them tagging the sky,
graffiti defying gravity.

They are what I look forward to
all day and all year.
Other planes are bigger
but none compare
to these darting beauties.

Fast like freedom,
now you see them,
now they're gone
but not quite, the sky is blue
but also red and white.

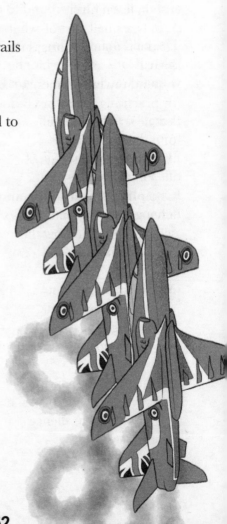

I'm so excited to start high school,
I spend hours and hours practising
my singing in my room.

I soon learn music
is only a small part of what my new
school is about: sports is the bigger
focus.
I spend my lunchtimes in the library
or practising guitar or clarinet
but never play football
or go near the cage
of boys and balls.

Choir meets on Tuesday and Thursday
after school. Mr and Mrs Evans
seem different to how they were
at my audition.

Mrs Evans is strict now.
'We're not here to talk,
just to sing,' she says.
Mr Evans doesn't use sheet music:

he knows all the songs. But
in between playing piano, he just stares
straight ahead in silence.
Emotionless.

No one at my school knows
that it's my birthday today.
I eat a packet of Party Rings to celebrate
in the toilets at lunch. I feel
invisible. I know if I keep my head down
then I can look forward to star-gazing,
peacefully, with Uncle B this evening.

After school, I'm walking behind Alistair
out of the school gates.

'Hey, choir boys!' comes a shout
from one of two bigger boys behind us.
Their grey blazers fit them better
than my over-sized one that Mum says
I'll grow into.

Alistair is a soprano and sings solos
when we perform in school assembly.
But outside choir he is quiet.
He has long hair that covers
half of his face.

They don't say why
we're supposed to fight,
only that if we don't hit each other
they will kick the shit out of us both.

'What's it gonna be, choir boys?'
the bigger of the two says, with a hiss
at the end of 'boys'.

Unlikely gladiators,
a crowd gathers, pushing us closer:
'Fight! Fight! Fight!'
A familiar chorus around here
but not one I'd ever chosen to sing.

I think of running.
I think of taking a beating.
But suddenly I feel this force within me.
Fight or flight?
I grab Alistair's hair with my left hand
and drag him around the circle two,
three times, then lift his head up
to see his long hair part to make way
for his pretty face and slap him hard
with my right hand, down to the ground.

The two bigger boys start shouting,
'Kick him! Kick him!'
His hair has fallen back
over his face now. He curls himself
into a ball. He looks so small,
like a chick just hatched from an egg.

I feel sick and ashamed. I want my mum.
'No!' I shout as I turn and
face the two who tower over me. I push
my way between the two boys and run and run
and don't stop until I reach the train station
where I throw up, rainbow violently,
on the platform.

When I get home Uncle B has bought me
my own telescope.

After dinner, I wash the dishes
while Mum puts Anna to bed,
and Uncle B sets it up and takes it out
into the garden.

It is almost as tall as me,
with the tripod fully extended.
The three legs are silver,
the tube of the telescope is white
and the lenses are black.

Uncle B adjusts it to the right height so I can
look down the lens. First, I look at the moon
and its craters. Then I look for constellations.
'The Plough. Orion. Pegasus,' I tell Uncle B,
proudly.

Uncle B says, 'Pegasus, the horse with wings
in Greek mythology, was born after the
beheading of Medusa, when a drop of
her blood fell to Earth.'

I silently wonder why
there is no constellation just for Medusa,
only her severed head with snakes for hair
dangling in Perseus's left-hand grip,
with his sword in his right hand, raised high.

When Uncle B leaves
and the stars are put away,
I think of Alistair.
His pretty face and long hair.

'Mummy,' I say, and go into the kitchen
where she is drying the dishes.

'Some older boys made me have a fight
with another boy from choir. He didn't do
anything to me but they told me I had to.
I only hit him once and then ran away.
I don't like the way boys get bigged up
for being violent. There's so much fighting
at my school. At primary school it was just
play fighting but now they're not playing.'

She puts the tea towel over her shoulder,
a hand on her hip and the other on the edge
of the sink. 'Some older boys told you to hit
someone? And you just did it?' She looks
shocked. I feel shame all over again.

'They surrounded us shouting, "Fight! Fight!"
I don't want to go back to choir.' I cry.
'I don't want to stay at that stupid school.'

'You're lucky it's your birthday,' Mum says.
'Just go to bed. Get out of my sight.'

I go to fold up my telescope to take
to my room and escape to the stars.

'Leave your telescope.'

I'm stuck here
with my shame.

Flamingos   fighting
can look just like kissing,
pecking beak-to-beak. Freeze
frame and you may see a love
heart in the shape of their
two necks arching out
and together
again.

The next day, after school,
Uncle B's BMW is waiting
outside the gate.

When I get in, he says,
'Your mum tells me
you've been fighting at school
and you want to move.'

'Yeah, that's right.'
I sink in my seat. 'People are looking.
Can we get out of here, please?'

Uncle B starts his engine.
'Are you being bullied?'
He takes a hand off the wheel
and places it on my shoulder.

'No.' I shrug him off. But I want it to stay.
'But I don't want to stay here.
It's all just fighting and football.
I want to go to a school with girls.'

In Uncle B's rearview mirror,
I watch that school disappear.

The second year of high school, I move
to a Church of England comprehensive
closer to home. A change from the all-boys
school last year. God grants me girls again.

On my first day, I'm told by Mr Casey
to sit next to Daisy Andrews.
Her name is before mine in the register.
When I hear her name, I know mine will follow.
Daisy doesn't say, 'Yes, sir,' or 'Yes, miss,'
when her name is called; she just says, 'Yeah.'
None of the teachers tell her off for this,
no one seems to notice. *I notice you, Daisy.*

Daisy Andrews reminds me of the Barbie
Goddess of Beauty that I never had. She is
slim, has dark eyes and long, dark, curly hair.
She looks like Selena Gomez but she is not
popular, for some reason I can't figure out.

In English class, I pluck up the courage
to ask Daisy: 'Who are you friends with?'
She replies: 'No one, they're all idiots.'

Talking to Daisy is like walking on eggshells.
I am curious what might have broken her.
She doesn't seem mean. She seems hurt.

In maths, I notice red-haired Rowan
at the desk in front of us. Rowan looks like
if Ed Sheeran was handsome. He's wearing
the correct uniform but makes it look scruffy.

I whisper to Daisy: 'Do you fancy anyone
in the school?'

She replies, 'No.' Pauses. 'Do you?'

I smile and shake my head. I'm not ready
to tell her. Rowan turns around and
smiles at me. *Did he hear my whisper?*

After school, when I get on the bus,
I spot Daisy sitting towards the back,
her Doc Marten boots up on the seat
in front. Even though we're the same
age, Daisy seems older than twelve.

'Hey, Daisy,' I say softly,
'do you reckon I can sit next to you?'
She moves her bag from the seat next to her
onto her lap.

'Yeah,' she replies, 'but I'm reading
so just don't talk to me.'
She gets back to *The Curious Incident
of the Dog in the Night-Time.*
I sit in silence next to Daisy.

Laughter and chatter rattles around
the rest of the bus but I feel a strange
sort of safety in this silence with Daisy.

Daisy continues reading her book
and I am reading her. *Can I trust her?*

'Bye, Daisy. See you tomorrow.'
'Yeah.'

The next day, as the bell goes
at the end of history class, I ask Daisy,
'Wanna get lunch together?'
I feel like she needs the company
as much as me.

'Do you have a packed lunch?' asks Daisy.
'No.' I pause. 'I get free school meals.'
'Well,' she says, 'you can sit with me after
you've eaten. I'll be in **B24**. Bring a book.'

I don't have a book but I think I might have
a new friend. I'm finishing my lunch, wolfing it
down extra quickly in the canteen. I need to
go to the library and pick up a book before I
go to **B24** to meet Daisy.

But then some girls join me. Two in front
and one next to me. The girl next to me
wears glasses, her blonde hair in a ponytail.

'Hey, I'm Grace,' says the blonde,
then points. 'This is Faith and Destiny.'
Faith and Destiny smile and Faith says, 'Hey.
You're the new boy, Michael, right?'
They both have their hair tied back as well.

Destiny is black and her hair is straightened.
Faith looks mixed like me, her hair is slicked
down to the scrunchy she wears, and then it puffs out at
the back like a halo.

I can't tell if it's just because I've eaten
my lunch too quickly or if I'm feeling
something like dread. I decide to swallow
that feeling. 'That's me,' I say, finishing up
my sponge cake. 'Nice to meet you.'

Grace asks, 'So why are you new?
Why did you leave your last school?'

I pause, remembering it. 'I had a fight.'
Destiny: 'Oh-em-gee! Were you expelled?'
Faith: 'Are you a bad boy, Michael?'
Grace: 'Don't be shy, Michael, tell us.'

I lie. 'I was just defending this boy,
Alistair, who was being picked on
by these two older boys for being in the choir.
I don't know what came over me,
I just went into this rage. I broke
one of their noses and gave the other
one a black eye and even though
I was the good guy, I still got expelled.'
'That's so unfair,' says Faith.
'Sooo unfair,' repeats Destiny.

In science, Daisy's silence feels different.
'I waited for you in **B24**,' she mutters.

I feel myself getting hot. 'I'm so sorry.
I totally forgot.'

Daisy turns away. 'Don't worry about it.'

I feel like I need to say
something
to make her talk to me.

'I didn't forget.
I mean, I got distracted.
These girls
started speaking to me
in the canteen.
Grace, Faith and Destiny.
Do you know them?'

'Yeah,' replies Daisy. 'They're mean.'

'Oh, really? They seem really cool.'

'Figures. They're only nice to boys.'

For the rest of my first week,
I eat in the canteen with Grace,
Faith and Destiny for half of lunch break.
They're in my year but different classes.
They gossip about other girls
and crush over boys. I laugh
when I think Grace wants a laugh,
or add a third echo in agreement with
whatever is being agreed upon.
I don't really listen to what they say.

For the second half of lunch break,
I go to **B24** and sit next to Daisy
and read in silence.

Daisy finishes *The Curious Incident*
and begins *The Fault in Our Stars*.
I read one book, *The Complete Collected
Poems of Maya Angelou*, for the whole week
and the following week, too.
Taking my time.

Maya Angelou has written autobiographies;
Mum has them all but when I try to read
them I get jumbled up and lose my place.
When I read her poems I always know where
I am. This poem. This page.

I'm inspired by Maya Angelou,
so I try to write my first poem
in the back of my maths book:

Maya Angelou

Maya Angelou's words
are so clear. She writes about love
and standing up for yourself
in the face of inequality.

Even though

she's American,
her words speak to me.

Her poetry is everything
I hope mine could be
one day, for somebody.

Even if

that somebody is me.

After school, I go to watch a fight
with Grace, Faith and Destiny.

They push to the front
and when we get there we see Kieran
from our year land a knock-out right-hook
to a boy from another school. Kieran is known
for fighting and football.
He makes me nervous. He makes me think
of my previous school.

His rival falls to the ground.
Everyone watching from our school
begins to chant, 'Kieran! Kieran! Kieran!'

This fight has nothing to do with me
but my
breathing
gets
funny.

'Kieran is so fit. Don't you think?' asks Grace.

I gulp for air.

'Oh my gosh, Grace. Shut up!' says Destiny.

'I'm not asking you,' says Grace.
'I'm asking *Michael*. Do you think
Kieran is fit, *Michael*?'

I wonder, *Is Kieran fit or is he frightening?*

Kieran is tall and black,
he has short hair with a fade.
He looks our way, he smiles and waves.

'I suppose,' I manage to say breathlessly.

Faith giggles.

'Oh-em-gee! Yuck!' says Destiny.

'Are you gay?' asks Grace.

There goes my breath again.

'You know that it's a sin?' says Faith.

Yes, I know. But I say nothing.

I skip lunch the following day
and go straight to **B24** to sit with Daisy. Relief
washes over me.

'I don't know what to say, Michael. I already
told you they were mean.'

'I know you did. I should have listened.
I'm sorry,' I say.

'That's okay. Anyway, are you gay?'

'Yes,' I say. *Finally, we're gonna talk about it.*

'Cool,' she says, and goes back to her book.

I thought she would ask me
how I knew and I could tell her
about my crush on Rowan.

'Wanna come to my house for dinner?' I ask.
'My mum's making shepherd's pie.'

'Okay,' says Daisy. She doesn't look up
but I notice a small smile forming on her lips.
'Can I read my book now?'

At the bus stop after school,
Grace confronts Daisy and me.

Faith and Destiny stand behind her
with their arms crossed, scowling.

'Queerdo and weirdo. Why are you *always*
together? Are you two girlfriends or
boyfriends?'

'Neither, not that it would be any of your
business,' I reply.

Daisy stares Grace down, like Goddess Barbie
would, unblinking.

'So are you both gay?' asks Grace, sneering.
'We're not judging you.'

'Only God can judge you,' says Destiny.

'Yeah, only God,' repeats Faith, with a wink.

'Do you three share one brain?' asks Daisy,
as she pushes past them and gets on the bus.

'Go with your boyfriend,' Grace says to me.

When I get on the bus,
Daisy has already put her bag on the seat
next to her.

I laugh. 'I'm having déjà vu, Daisy! Move
the bag so I can sit down.'

'Just leave me alone, Michael.'

I stand over her, not moving. 'It's not my fault.'

'You hardly defended me, did you?'

'You can clearly defend yourself, Daisy.
What did you want me to say?'

'I don't know. Something. Anything.
Not just stand there and take abuse.'

'I said it was none of their business, didn't I?'
I look at her pleadingly.

The bus jolts forward, I grab the railing.

Daisy moves her bag, so I can sit down.

After a few stops in silence, I ask,
'Are you still coming to mine for dinner?'

'Of course I am, queerdo,' says Daisy.

'Shut up, weirdo.' I laugh and put my arm
around her and kiss her on the cheek.

'Daisy, are you Greek?' asks Mum,
while serving up the shepherd's pie.

Daisy laughs. 'I usually get asked
if I'm Spanish.'

Mum starts with her own version
of the Spanish Inquisition: 'Are you Spanish?'

'No. My dad is English,' says Daisy,
'and my mum is half-English, half-Jamaican.'

I remember Mum's speech about halves.
We never talked about quarters, but isn't that
what Daisy is?

'Michael and Anna's dads are Jamaican.
I'm Greek-Cypriot,' Mum says, proudly.
'You look like you could be my daughter.'

'Mummy,' says Anna, who has already started
eating, 'this tastes funny.'

'It's Quorn mince,' says Mum. 'I wanted to see
if you could tell the difference.'

Up in my room, after dinner,
I show Daisy the copy of *Cosmopolitan*
magazine I stole from Mum's room,
with Adam Levine on the cover.
'He's so fit, right?' I say to Daisy.

Bob Marley and Beyoncé watch over us
from my bedroom wall.

Excited to be breaking my silence,
I continue: 'I've got the biggest crush
on Rowan at school. He's not sexy
like Adam Levine but he's really cute,
and he's a bit random, like in drama
he really goes for it with different accents
and he's not shy to play girl characters
and then in maths he puts his hand up
and he always gets the answers right.
How can he be so talented and so clever?'

Daisy laughs as she examines the magazine,
then says, 'I'm not sure about Rowan
but yes to Adam Levine.'

Daisy starts coming round for dinner
at least two or three times a week.

She never invites me to her house;
she refers to it as 'the War Zone'.

She tells me, 'You're lucky
to have one parent. Two is a nightmare.'

She helps me and Anna with homework.

Mum calls Daisy her daughter
but as Daisy's breasts get bigger,
I find myself staring at them
when we sit in my bedroom
or even at school in **B24**.

I think about kissing her.
I know it would be wrong
to just kiss her.

I could just ask her.
Daisy, can I kiss you?

But I never do.

In the back of my maths book I write:

Divided by Love

Maths is the hardest class to focus in;
I have Daisy sitting next to me
and Rowan at the desk in front.
Rowan is so cute and Daisy is
equally so. I feel divided. I wish I could
just have a normal day at school.

In the back of my maths book I write:

How Gay Am I?

How gay am I? I wonder.
I know if I could choose
I would be with Rowan
but he's a mystery to me.

It's so easy with Daisy.
She's my best friend.
She's part of my family.
She's like a part of me.

At the start of the next maths class,
when Mrs Briggs gives out our books,
she puts three on our table: Daisy's, mine
and another new book in front of me.

I open it up and I see a pink Post-it note:
'FOR YOUR POETRY'.

It has lined rather than squared pages.
I close it quickly, hoping Daisy didn't see.

I feel so embarrassed Mrs Briggs has
read what I wrote about Daisy and Rowan.

Carefully, I rip out the poetry pages from
the back of my maths book and slip them

inside this new book. *My POETRY book.*

Daisy is off sick today
with period pains
and in drama class Rowan asks
to be my partner.

In our pairs, we all find a space
of our own in the drama studio.

We've been told to play a game
called, 'Yes, And!'

Whatever your partner says,
you're supposed to agree and add something.

I say to Rowan: 'We're going to the beach.'

Rowan says, 'Yes, and it's a nudist beach,
so we have to get naked.' He takes off his tie,
and swings it at crotch-level.

I laugh, and take off my tie, and swing it, too.

I say: 'Yes, and let's get in the water now.'

He says: 'Yes, and let's swim to that island,
over there.'

Rowan points,
and we swim past our classmates
all playing in their pairs
until we reach the corner of the drama studio
where the ceiling-to-floor-length black curtains
gather.

I say: 'Yes, and we've arrived on the island.'

He says: 'Yes, and it's night-time now.'
He goes behind the curtains.

I follow.

I say: 'Yes, and it's only the two of us here.'

He says: 'Yes, and…'

He steps closer, says again: 'Yes, and…'

The bell goes for the end of class.

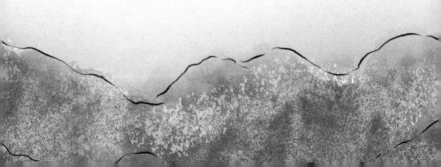

MICHAEL: Daisy!! Guess what!!

DAISY: What?

MICHAEL: Rowan almost kissed me!

DAISY: Almost?? How??

MICHAEL: In drama class but the bell went

DAISY: It doesn't count if it's in drama class

MICHAEL: Why not?

DAISY: He's just a show-off.
He loves attention

MICHAEL: And I love him!

DAISY:

I'm in my bathroom, getting ready
for the Year 9 school disco, when I notice
the first hairs above my top lip. I decide
to use Mum's razor from the side
of the bathtub. I know she uses it for her legs –
there are little dark hairs on it –
but a razor is a razor. I make
my first attempt at shaving. Moments later,
I have a symmetrical moustache
of blood from where I managed
to cut myself evenly on both sides.

When Daisy arrives in a glittery red dress,
I'm wearing nothing but my black boxer shorts,
sulking on my bed.

I wonder how that dress would look on me?
I think for a moment, before remembering
I'm feeling sorry for myself.

'Maybe we can put some concealer on it,'
says Daisy, reaching into her bag. Daisy has
started wearing make-up, but not too much.
She looks much older than fourteen.
I barely look twelve.

'No way,' I say,
'I'm not wearing make-up! I'd rather miss
the stupid disco.'
'That's a shame,' says Daisy.
'You might have had a dance, maybe even
a kiss with Rowan.'

Daisy lifts up the duvet
and we both slide in.
We spend the evening
watching prom movies
with happy endings.

I tell Mum I've decided to locs my hair.
Mum doesn't mind; she says: 'Do whatever
makes you happy, Michael. As long
as you focus on your GCSEs.'

The hairdresser says,
'Because your hair is so soft,
I have to wrap it up with synthetic hair
and it will locs up underneath.
People won't be able to tell to look at it.
Every day you must keep twisting
the roots – as it grows, the synthetic
hair will fall out and you'll have locs
underneath. It will look like locs
straight away and it will become
real locs over time.'

After the hairdresser,
I go to visit Granny B
to show her my locs,
hoping she will see me
as more Jamaican.

She says, 'Me nah like it,
Mikey. Back a yard only Rasta man
ave dis. Yuh tun Rasta?'

I don't answer. I don't know much
about Rastafarians but I like how
the hairstyle looked on Bob Marley.

Granny B kisses her teeth
and puts a plate of food down
in front of me.

Curried goat and rice and peas.
Then she places a twenty pound note
next to my plate.

She says, 'Tek dis fi de barber shop.
Cut it off, Mikey. Cut it off.'
I eat my dinner silently and accidentally
on purpose elbow the twenty to the floor,
hoping Granny will hoover it up.

Dear Bob Marley,

What's it like to be mixed but accepted
as black?

What's it like for your work to be known
around the world?

What's it like to survive death through
your work?

What's it like to not know your father
but still know yourself?

One lunchtime in **B24**, Daisy and I
share cold but tasty shepherd's pie
from my black Tupperware box.
I ask Daisy, 'Why do you say you're white?
Are you ashamed of being mixed?'

Daisy snaps back:
'My mum is mixed
but she doesn't even say so.
She's only talked to me about it once.
I've never met her Jamaican family.
I'm not ashamed but I have nothing
to claim, nothing handed down to me.
It's not something people can see
to look at me; maybe if I'm with my mum
but I never am. On my own
I just look like a white girl with a tan
and that suits me just fine, I don't want
to explain myself to people. I've seen
how you have to do it. How people ask
you questions like they have the right
to see your family tree. I don't want that.
I just want to be me.'

I don't want to make her any more angry,
so I don't say, *You're hiding
a part of yourself.*

COMING OUT

Dear Rowan,

I've liked you for so long.
You're always so smiley.
You seem so carefree.
I don't know you very well
but I really like what I see.
I like your ginger hair, your freckles.
You're cool but kind of goofy.
You're so confident in drama.
I wish we had more classes together.
Maybe we would know each other better.
In drama we're always pretending
to be someone else,
maybe that's school in general?
I don't want to pretend with you.
I like you.
Although I don't really know you,
I'd like to.
So please write back
or tell me when you see me,
will you go out with me?

Michael

With letter in hand,
I look for Rowan.

He's easy to find.
The only ginger boy
in the whole school.

He's a constant flame.
A candle always lit.

I call out his name.
He turns, flicking his red mane
out of his eyes.

I'm reminded
of that pretty boy, Alistair,
with the long hair
at my last school.
Were we picked
and made to fight
because those bigger
boys saw something
we hadn't realised?

Rowan is facing me
now and I feel that
familiar feeling.

No one is chanting,
Fight! Fight! Fight!
But I hear it anyway.

I don't want to fight,
I want the opposite.

It's a smiling stand-off.
I'm smiling and saying
nothing. He's smiling
but his smile is fading.

I think of our almost-kiss
and it gives me courage.

I hold out my hand.
'This is for you,' I shout,
and kids have started to stop
and stare but I don't care.

'What is it?'

'It's a letter asking if you'll go out with me.'

Shit! Why did I say that so loudly?
The onlookers giggle.

'Oh, right,' he says. 'This is awkward.'

'I'm sorry,' I say, realising
I've got it completely wrong.

'I'm sorry,' says Rowan.

'It's okay,' I say. 'It's okay,' I repeat,
even though it's not okay.

And the letter drops to my feet.
I look down but don't pick it up.

Instead I pick up speed
and head to my next class,
thanking God it isn't drama.

In the corridor,
after double R.E.,
Mr Casey asks if I'm okay –
I don't seem myself today, apparently.
I tell him about my letter to Rowan
and that I think I'm gay.
I ask him if I'm going to Hell.
He tells me about relationships
between men in the Bible.
He tells me that male friendship is natural.
I tell him I'm not talking about friendship.
He says I shouldn't have sex yet.
He has a point, I guess: I'm only fifteen
but sometimes it feels like
everyone else is doing it.
Anyway, that's not what I wanted from Rowan.
I just thought maybe he might like me.
But I was wrong.

I'm in **B24**, waiting for Daisy at lunchtime.
Rereading the first line of *The Color Purple*:
'You better not never tell nobody but God.'

We're studying the book for English.
I've watched the movie seven times
but I never get past the first line when
I open the book.

Kieran knocks at the door, even though
it's open. I feel that fight or flight feeling.

He walks in towards me
and my heart is racing.
'I saw you drop this,' says Kieran,
placing my letter to Rowan in the open
palms of the book's pages.
'And I didn't think you'd want
anyone to read it.'
He pauses. 'I read it, though –
it's really sweet.'

I'm embarrassed and confused
and still a bit afraid.
'Are you okay?' asks Kieran.

'Yes, I'm gay,' I say, ready for him to hit me.

He laughs. 'No, idiot, I said are you *okay*?'

'Oh. Yeah. I think so. No,' I say.

Don't cry, Michael. Please don't cry,
I say to myself, but it's too late.

I don't know why he's being so nice.

He puts his arm around me and says,
'Don't worry, you can't score every time
but you still gotta take the shot.
Respect for taking the risk, bro.
I've got a question for you: Why did you
ask out the whitest boy in school?
Why not give a brother a chance?'

I laugh, through my tears. 'You're funny.'

'Yeah,' Kieran sighs, 'so are you.
I should go but if anyone gives you any trouble,
you let me know.'
He squeezes my shoulder,
walks to the door.

He turns back. 'Did you know
the first openly gay professional footballer
was Justin Fashanu? He was the first
black footballer to get a million quid
transfer fee, which is nothing today,
but in the eighties it was a really big deal.'

Kieran hovers at the door for a second more,
then leaves.

I take out my phone.
I Google: 'Justin Fashanu'.
What Kieran said is true
but it looks like life was hell
after he came out. He killed himself.
I wonder if Kieran knows that?

I have English after lunch
and when I walk in, I'm sure
people are talking about me.
Daisy's chair is empty.
I haven't seen or heard from her all day.

When class starts, I resign myself
to the fact that Daisy's not here today.
But then she bursts in.
'I'm sorry I'm late, sir. It won't happen again.'

When she sits down next to me,
she whispers, 'This is for you.'
She slides me
a folded sheet of paper with my name on.

Dear Michael,

I hope you're okay.
I'm sorry I didn't get to read your letter.
When you left, Kieran picked it up.
He told me I was cold-hearted.
I'm sorry.
I was taken by surprise.
If it helps you to know,
I'm bisexual. Are you?
I thought you and Daisy were together.
I've got a girlfriend.
She's at a different school.
I reckon I love her.
You seem wonderful.
And brave.
I'm sure you'll find someone.

See you in drama.

Rowan :)

Daisy wants to hang out
after school but I want to go straight
home. I'm thinking about what it means
to be out to my whole school.

I'm thinking about Rowan.
I'm thinking about Kieran.
I'm thinking about going to Hell when I die
and a living Hell on Earth.

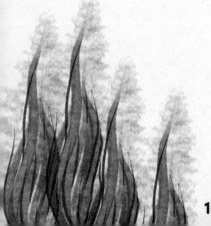
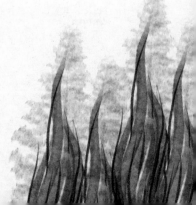

I never wear gloves when washing
the dishes. I use more Fairy Liquid
than I need to. I stare into the bubbles.

My bare hands in the water; it's not
scalding but hot enough that I feel
something. My hands. Nothing else.

My actions are automatic. I don't
realise I'm crying until Mum comes
in and asks, 'What's the matter?'

'I asked someone out today,' I say.

'What did she say?' asks Mum.

'He said no, Mummy. HE said NO!'

It's gloriously dramatic, the way
I throw myself to the floor and begin
to sob. Mum is the only audience
I need for this moment. It's the rejection,
it's the relief, it's a rejoicing of sorts.

Mum kneels down next to me

and I curl onto her lap

and she rubs my back,

and she says, 'It's OK,'

and I shout, 'I know it is!'

and she silently rubs my back,

then she says, 'You have to be careful.

You have to use condoms.

Because of HIV.

You know?'

'I know, Mummy,' I say. 'I know.'

I look at Kieran differently, appreciating
his looks and football skills for the first time.
He becomes my imaginary boyfriend.

It's comforting. We don't have
any classes together but at lunchtimes
he waves at me from the football cage;
at least I think he's waving at me –
he could be waving at Daisy.

'Do you fancy Kieran?' I ask Daisy.

'No,' she says. 'I don't fancy black boys.'

It's another one of those things she says
that I don't know how to respond to.
If we weren't friends I'd think she was racist.
Can you be racist when you're a quarter black?

How could anyone not fancy Kieran?
He has a perfect smile, the fade in his hair
always looks fresh. He never looks scruffy;
even after a whole lunch hour of playing
football, he doesn't even break a sweat.

I imagine standing at the entrance
to the football cage, watching Kieran play
and when he scores a goal he runs over
to kiss me, in celebration. And it's normal.

I imagine sitting at the back of the bus
with him and all the other black boys
on the way home from school,
and not in the middle, with Daisy.

Nothing changes about their laughter
and banter as Kieran puts his arm around me.

Our P.E. teacher wears
rainbow laces
on his football boots.

The two things I enjoy
about football
are watching Kieran play,
and how our teacher's laces
say to me:
'It's okay to be gay.'

If Kieran was my boyfriend,
would Mum let him stay over?
Would we wait until sixteen?
Would we wait until marriage?

How Christian is Kieran?
When God made Kieran,

did He make him for me?
I imagine us in Eden –

two black boys in Paradise,
naked, no fig leaves.
Adam and Eve are long-gone,
so Kieran and Michael

inherit the garden
and the serpent is forgotten
and the fruit on the tree
of knowledge has gone rotten.

SWEET SIXTEEN

Sometimes I find notes in my school bag.
They are quotes from the Bible.

'You shall not lie with a male
as with a woman; it is an abomination.'
(Leviticus 18:22)

'If a man lies with a male as with a woman,
both of them have committed an abomination;
they shall surely be put to death.'
(Leviticus 20:13)

I don't tell Daisy or anyone about them.
I never let my bag out of my sight
and yet the notes keep turning up.

They shout,

'Batty bwoy!'

And again,

'Batty bwoy!'

I'm on my own street
in Wembley. I'm afraid
but I look towards them
for a second.
Four laughing kids:
two Asian boys,
one black boy
and one white girl,
around my sister's age.
I don't recognise them
but I recognise this patois
so carelessly/violently
flung in my direction.

'Batty bwoy!' Meaning
less-than-man who is
penetrated by or penetrates
another less-than-man.
I realise this phrase is sexual.
This phrase is about sex.
It's like shouting out,

'You have bum sex!'

I've heard it in music,
in songs from Jamaica
that call for gay men
to be killed.

When I get home
I'm shaking. I tell Mum:
'They were much younger
than me, probably Anna's age,
but it was scary.
How do they know I'm gay?
Can people just see it?'

Mum puts her hands
on my shoulders and
looks me in the eyes.
'People are cruel, Michael.
Kids are cruel. Adults are cruel.
It's just a part of life.'

I thought she would tell me
how awful what they said was.
I thought maybe she would call the police.

Instead she quietly asks,
'Have you told your sister?
Does Anna know that you're gay?'

I assume Anna knows
from how we dance
to Beyoncé together
and watch *RuPaul's Drag Race*.

I guess I could be straight
and do those things.

I call her downstairs
and say:
'I need to tell you,
I'm gay.'

She laughs. 'I know.' Then asks,
'Have you got a boyfriend?'

DAISY: HAPPY BIRTHDAY!
Let's go out after school?

MICHAEL: I can't. Soz

DAISY: I know you're funny about your birthday
but it would be nice to hang out. Cinema?

DAISY: My treat. There's a really cool-looking
film I want to see called *The Lobster*

MICHAEL: I'm going for a drive with Uncle B

MUM: I'm making shepherd's pie
tonight as a birthday treat

MICHAEL: That stopped being my favourite
years ago

MICHAEL: I'm going to the cinema with Daisy

MUM: Okay. Have fun. I'll have it ready
for when you're back

At school, I sit in the loos.
In my bag are the condoms
that Mum bought me,
along with a new, thick, black
notebook and special pen.
The notebook is Moleskine
and the pen is Cross.
I'm nervous bringing them to school
in case I lose them.
I'm nervous taking the condoms
in case someone sees them.
I download an app
that allows me to talk
to gay guys in the area.
I arrange to meet a guy
called Alex after school.
He sends me a photo.
He looks friendly:
a big smile, white teeth,
blue eyes, a bit pink in the face.
He says I can't come
to his place but he knows
somewhere we can go.

We're kneeling on a patch of
grass between two graves, kissing
with tongues, our mouths dry
from the spliff we just smoked.
My first spliff, my first proper kiss.
Alex said he's nineteen but he looks older.
Maybe it's his grey suit, the jacket
hanging on one gravestone,
my black school blazer on the other.
Maybe it's his stubble – he was clean-
shaven in his photo.

Alex has his hand in the small of my back.
It feels like the only thing holding me upright.

He stops. 'Do you do poppers?'
I close my eyes and imagine
tiny plastic cannons about to be pulled,
balloons about to drop from the ceiling
and my Teenage Mutant Ninja Turtles
birthday cake from when I turned six.

I'm high on weed, about to lose
my virginity in a graveyard. He hands me
a small glass bottle full of liquid.
I unscrew the top. 'Do I drink it?'
'No, you hold it under your nose, like this,
and inhale; it helps you to relax.'

I follow his instructions.
A chemical explosion in my brain,
streamers burst forth into a tangled
rainbow, then all fades to black.

When I wake his eyes reflect me
as a zombie rising from a grave.
I feel like an empty plastic cannon,
party debris, balloon shrapnel.

When I get back home, cold shepherd's pie
is waiting for me. Mum doesn't ask
about the mud on my trousers.
My red eyes. My missing school blazer.

Lying in bed that night,
I imagine all the ways
Alex might have hurt me
when I was passed out.
He didn't hurt me, but
he so easily could have
killed me and we were
already in a graveyard.
I was stupid to meet him
without telling anyone.
It was exciting at the time
but now my imagination
won't stop showing me
all the horrible things
someone could do to me.
Whether I'm passed out
or not, they could force me.
I'm not big. I'm not strong.
Meeting a man is not
a good idea. Just because
I can, it doesn't mean I'm ready
to lose my virginity
to a stranger.
I decide to delete the app
to protect myself.

MICHAEL: Hey

DAISY: Hey! 2 mins left of your birthday
How was your evening?

~~**MICHAEL:** So awful. I did something stupid~~

MICHAEL: It was okay. Uncle B said to say hey

DAISY: 👋
I went to see that movie Lobster
It was so weird
People got turned into animals
If they couldn't find a relationship

MICHAEL: That sounds messed up!

DAISY: Yh. But they get to pick the animal

MICHAEL: What animal would you be?

DAISY: I think maybe a flamingo. You?

MICHAEL: I don't know. Maybe a turtle

Broken / Home

Because the turtle carries
its home on its back,
it does not have to search for one.
It is born with a soft shell
that hardens as it grows.
The turtle's backbone is part
of its shell, meaning an accident
or attack could break the turtle's back,
leaving the turtle with a broken
home it cannot escape from.

LEVENTIS

Mum is going through a phase
of making us any meal on request:
jerk chicken or curried goat with rice and peas,
ackee and salt fish, stuffed vine leaves,
shepherd's pie, Sunday roast.

Mum buys me and Anna games consoles,
phones, clothes, anything she can afford,
and, when she can't afford it, she borrows
money to send me to hip-hop dance class
and Anna to ballet and, now, to take us
on our first holiday.

Mum bursts into the kitchen.
'I've got a surprise for you all!'

We're slumped at the table.
Daisy and I are taking a break
from our A level revision.

Daisy is helping Anna
with her much easier homework,
and I'm writing a poem.

'I've just spoken to your dad, Daisy.
He says he'll pay for your ticket
to come with us to Cyprus for Easter.'

'We're going on holiday?' shouts Anna,
bolting upright excitedly, slamming
both hands on the kitchen table. Daisy
catches Anna's pencil as it rolls off the edge.

I sit back in my chair and
close my notebook. 'Who's paying
for our tickets, Mummy?'

'Trevor gave some money for Anna
and Uncle B for you.'

The Men Who Are Not My Dad

My sister's dad	is not my dad.
Uncle B	is not my dad.
Our Father, in Heaven	is not my dad.
My R.E. teacher	is not my dad.
My P.E. teacher	is not my dad.
My English teacher	is not my dad.
My drama teacher	is not my dad.
Bob Marley	is not my dad.
Idris Elba	is not my dad.
Will Smith	is not my dad.
Jay Z	is not my dad.
My own father	is not my dad.

Anna jumps out of her seat and
dances around the table. 'We're going
on holiday! We're going on holiday!'

'Thank you!' says Daisy to my mum,
hugging her.

'Thanks, Mummy,' I say from my seat.

Sometimes
I think Mum loves Daisy as much as us.
Sometimes maybe more than me.

I'm angry Mum didn't ask me
if I wanted Daisy to come on holiday.
I would have said yes
but I didn't get a chance to decide.

Mum, Anna and Daisy
go shopping
for swimming costumes.
I decide to stay home.
'Just get me black trunks,
no Speedos,' I say.

Whilst they're gone
I Google 'Speedos'
and the first page
of results brings up
pictures of Tom Daley.
I'm still looking at them
when Mum, Anna and
Daisy return.

Mum hands me a shopping bag.
'Thanks, Mummy,' I say.
'You're welcome.' Mum giggles.
'I'm gonna start packing,
one week to go! Anna,
come and help me pack.'

Mum and Anna run out the room,
holding hands and laughing.
I look in the bag to find
the tiniest
pair

of bright pink Speedos I've ever seen.

Daisy bursts out laughing.
'It's not even funny!' I shout,
throwing the tiny, pink piece
of material right at Daisy's face.
'Who wasted our money
on a stupid joke like that?'

Daisy takes the Speedos
off her face, still laughing,
and takes some black trunks
out of her own shopping bag
and hands them to me.
'You should've seen your face!'
says Daisy, still creasing up.

'You should have seen yours,'
I reply, preparing my killer blow:
'Much improved when covered up.
What am I supposed to do with *these*?'
I hold up the pink Speedos.

When Daisy heads home, I go
to my room and push my bed
across to barricade the door.
I fling off my clothes. Squeeze
into the Speedos. I'm no Tom Daley
but I like what I see in my full-length mirror.
I turn to check out my butt,
twerk a little, giggle.

Uncle B drives us to the airport.
He and Mum chat the whole journey.
Anna and Daisy are in the back
seat next to me, Daisy in the middle.
I stare out of the window at nothing
in particular for the whole journey.

Anna and Daisy listen to Little Mix
from Daisy's phone, one earpiece
each. They sing along to 'Black Magic'.
I like the song but I don't join in.

I always thought Uncle B would
take me on my first holiday.
I thought it would be Jamaica.

As I'm helping him unload our bags
from the boot and onto the trolley,
I say, 'Thank you for giving my mum
the money.' I don't say, *I wish
you were my dad instead of him.*

On the plane we have three seats
next to each other and one across
the aisle. Anna wants the window
seat and Mum to sit beside her.

I tell Daisy to sit next to Mum and
I take the seat across the aisle with
two strangers, who are not strangers
to each other.

The couple kiss for the whole flight.
They only break from kissing to speak
in Greek, and I only know a few words
Mum taught me. It becomes background
noise to me – I hear the word *agape*,
which means 'love' and *agape mou*,
which means 'my love'.

We arrive at my grandparents'
house in Larnaca in a taxi late at night.
Things are familiar but different.
Even my name is different here.
My grandparents call me 'Michalis',
which is a more Greek way to say 'Michael'.

Grandma says, '*Éla, agape mou.*'
Gesturing me to come to the table.
She has made stuffed vine leaves,
like the ones Mum makes, except
these have real meat and not tasteless
soya mince. Mum moans,
repeating, 'I told her I don't eat meat.'
Shaking her head, as she
transfers stuffed vine leaves
from her plate onto mine.

There are enough bedrooms
at my grandparents' house for Daisy
and me to have our own rooms,
if Mum and Anna share.

Grandma comes up and
helps us get settled.

Mum continues to be short-tempered
and dismissive with Grandma,
the way I am sometimes short-tempered
and dismissive with Mum.

I can't work out what Mum
and Grandma are saying for the most part,
because they speak in Greek.

Hearing Mum speak another language
and be so stroppy like this,
she is like a different person.
Like she has become her teenage
self again. The girl she was before me.
The girl from the last millennium.

On the beach the next day,
Daisy has taken Anna
to get ice cream.

Strangers
shout, 'Bob Marley!'
The first few times I laugh and wave
but after a while I just roll my eyes.

A girl in a pink bikini
comes up to me and touches my hair:
'Xereis na milas ellinika?'

'Excuse me?' I say, in shock
as I back away from her.

She repeats, in English,
'Do you speak Greek?'

'No, I can't speak Greek.'

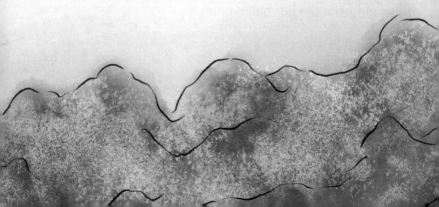

She says, 'You're from Jamaica.'
Is she asking me or telling me?

'*Leventis,*' she says to her friend,
who I hadn't noticed.

Before I have a chance to respond,
the friend looks me up and down
and nods. They giggle,
link arms and walk into the sea.

'*Leventis,*' I repeat, so I don't forget.

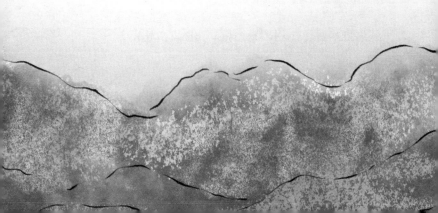

'Mummy, what does *"leventis"* mean?'

She laughs,
looking up from her book and squinting.
'Who said that to you?'

I shuffle to the right
to block the sun from her eyes. 'Some girl,
just now.' I point towards the sea but I can't tell
one pink bikini from another.

'It means "handsome man" or it could mean
"beautiful boy". And it can also mean "brave".'

I'm shocked that it's not something bad.

'*Leventis*,' I repeat,
once again. Handsome man, beautiful boy
or brave. *But am I any of these things?*
Maybe to a Greek-Cypriot girl on a beach.

But where are the boys who see me this way?

Leventis. Does it really translate into English?

I don't feel handsome,
I don't feel beautiful
and I don't feel brave.

Apart from the cigarette
butts this beach is perfect.
I've got sunblock on but I
don't think I really need it.
It's like one of our better
summer days in England:
warm, not too hot to handle.
But we're a long way from
the pebbles of Brighton.

Anna and I build our first
proper sandcastle together.
We dig a moat around it,
pour in the Mediterranean.

Daisy is revising
on her sunbed, surrounded
by books and index cards.
I was planning to revise, too.
But now we're here it seems silly.

Daisy and I are both applying
to do English at uni,
but not to any of the same places.

I shout over to Daisy: 'Don't you think
it could be fun if you came to Brighton?'

Daisy looks up and says bluntly,
'You know Brighton is of no interest to me.'

Anna giggles, and repeats,
'You know Brighton is of no interest to me.'

Daisy says, 'Oi, are you making fun of me?'

She reaches down and grabs a handful
of sand and throws it in our direction.

Anna laughs and throws sand back at Daisy.

'Stop it!' says Mum, caught in the crossfire.

Mum is sunbathing, reading
It by Stephen King.
I watched the movie years ago
with Trevor. He told me I was brave
because I wasn't afraid
of any of the movies he showed me.

In *It* there's an evil clown
called Pennywise, who makes
children see their worst fear.

I lie back on the sand
and look up to the sky
and can no longer see the outlines
of Mum, Anna or Daisy,
and I realise with all the knowing in the world
that my worst fear is
to be without my family
– that includes Daisy.

I crawl unnoticed behind
Mum's sunbed and whisper
a line from the movie in her ear:
'We all float down here.'
Mum screams, then laughs
and hits me with her book.
Anna laughs too, adding
another keep to our castle.

Mum brings me a magazine
from the beach shop:
Attitude, with
Tom Daley on the cover.
'The Body Issue.'

I've already looked
at *Attitude*'s website on my phone,
but when Mum hands me
the physical copy,
I feel like she's
giving me her blessing.

Inside the magazine,
the advice is to accept
and love your body,
no matter how you look.
I don't think about
my skinny physique often
but here I can't help
myself.

I don't know where to
look with all the nearly
naked men's bodies,
biceps, torsos, tiny
Speedos.

I think about my pink
Speedos. I packed them
secretly – maybe I could
come back to the beach in them later,
join all the men who know
who they are and don't mind
wearing tiny Speedos.

Mum looks me up and
down from her sunbed
and says, 'Maybe when
we get back to London
you could join my gym.'

Our second evening, we visit our great-aunt
for dinner. She points to Daisy first
and I can work out from Mum's hand
gestures that Mum is explaining Daisy
is not her child, but Anna and I are.

She doesn't speak any English but
she smiles and she feeds us. Black-eyed
beans and greens. This food, again, is familiar
but her words are not. Our great-aunt
refers to Anna and me as *'ta mávra'*.

Mum doesn't want to translate it but I insist.
'It means **"the black ones"**,
but not in a bad way.'

I don't know why Mum needed to say
not in a bad way, unless it *was* bad.

Daisy isn't seen as black like Anna and me.
Daisy looks down at her plate and doesn't
say anything.

Mum hardly speaks any Greek to us at home.
She has always said she wanted to fit in
and be British. Here in Cyprus, Anna and I
can't access family conversations without
her translations.

Mum, Anna and Daisy go shopping
the next day, so I stay at the house with my
grandparents.

Sitting out on the porch with Grandad
I look over my revision for the first time
since we got here.

Lighting a cigarette,
Grandad asks, 'Are you studying hard?'

'Yes, Grandad.' Looking down
at my notes, which Daisy wrote for me,
I add guiltily, 'Daisy usually helps me.'

'She's your girlfriend?' he asks,
with a big smile.

'No, she's my best friend.'

'This is the same thing?' asks Grandad.

'Almost.' I smile.

Grandad goes back inside.
He draws my attention
to the news: the story, a black flamingo
has landed on the island.

An expert on screen
explaining it is the opposite
of an albino. 'Too much
melanin,' he says. Camera pans
the salt lake full of pink
but my eye is drawn
to that one black body
in the flamboyance.

The following evening.
My beach towel and shorts dry
on the balcony.

Couples on mopeds ride
past the house. Dogs walk
humans before dinner.

Grandad coughs violently,
then lights another cigarette.

Grandma calls us in to eat.

The black flamingo is on the news again.
I pick the dining chair facing the TV.

Grandad asks,
'Why does it matter if he's black?'
Adding, 'The other flamingos don't care.'

And I am certain what he's saying is:

'I love you.'

At Larnaca airport,
I see a pink flamingo stuffed toy in Duty Free.
Daisy takes the piss but I ask Mum
to buy it for me.

'Why don't I get that for Anna?'
'Fine, I'll get another one.' I return
with a second pink flamingo
but Mum is holding a bottle
of Jean Paul Gaultier's Le Male eau de toilette.

The bottle is blue, in the shape of a male body
with no arms, legs or head, just a toned torso
and bulging groin.

Mum says, 'I'm getting this for you,
the flamingo for Anna and this for Daisy,'
picking up a pink perfume bottle.

I put down the toy.

When we get home,
I place the blue bottle on my desk next
to my Lynx Africa, Vaseline and cocoa butter.

I take a shower,
wash off the last of the Mediterranean.

When I return to my bedroom,
my sister's flamingo toy
rests on my pillow.

In my dream that night, Kieran and I are
on TV together; we are a pair of black
flamingos.

The camera zooms out
and we're just two of many black flamingos
standing on the salt lake.

SHOWBUSINESS

The weekend before I turn seventeen,
Daisy and I go to the cinema
to see *Moonlight*.

Even though it's set in America,
I see something of myself
onscreen. I recognise what's missing
for them is also missing
for me. I recognise the longing
for a man, a father, a lover.

As the credits roll, Daisy and I stand
and put our coats on. It's dark but I recognise
Kieran, sitting two rows behind us.
I don't recognise the girl Kieran
has his arm around. I don't think he sees me.
I nudge Daisy. 'Look, it's Kieran.'

I think I'm too loud, as he looks our way.
Daisy and I link arms and scuttle out
as quick as we can without actually running.
We burst out laughing when we get outside.

Daisy says, 'That's cool that Kieran came
to see this film. Do you think that was his
girlfriend? It definitely looked like a date.'

It's my seventeenth birthday
and, even though it's a school night,
Mum is taking me, Anna and Daisy
on the Bakerloo line to Piccadilly Circus
to a theatre in the West End
to see a musical called *Kinky Boots*.

Mum tells me it was a film first. I've not seen it.
I've never seen anything like it.

Coming out of the theatre,
I ask Mum, 'Were there songs in the movie?'

'Yes, there were songs,' she says.

'And was the drag queen black in the movie?'

'Yes, the film was mostly the same.'

'Mummy!' I exclaim. 'Why did you never
show me this movie?'

'I don't know why, Michael, but did you
enjoy the show?'

'I loved it, Mummy!' I hug her and I never
want to let her go.

Anna interrupts: 'Mummy, why do you say "film"
but Michael says "movie"?'

Daisy laughs, putting her arm around Anna,
and says, 'You notice a lot for a nine-year-old,
don't you?'

Anna replies, 'I guess.'

I reach out my left arm in their direction
and pull them both into the hug.

'Would you ever do drag?' Daisy asks,
her arm in mine as we walk ahead
of Mum and Anna down Shaftesbury Avenue
towards Piccadilly Circus.

'What, for Halloween? You know I don't do
Halloween,' I reply.

'Not for Halloween,' says Daisy. 'In general,
for fun.'

'No, I don't think so. But watching it tonight
was the best thing ever!'

We squeeze into a Bakerloo line carriage.
A skeleton and a vampire
give up their seats for Anna and Mum.

Daisy and I stand surrounded
by a whole convent's worth of zombie nuns,
giggling and swigging from wine bottles
with handwritten sticky labels:
'Jesus Juice'. One of them offers
us her bottle and I look toward Mum,
who is looking at her phone, with Anna
already asleep tucked under her other arm.

I take a swig
and offer it to Daisy, who swigs, giggles and
says, 'Thanks.'

'Where are your costumes?' asks the Undead
Wife of Christ, taking her wine bottle back.

'I don't do Halloween,' I say.
Daisy chimes in, 'Today's his birthday.'

'What, really?' asks the wine-giver.
Without waiting for an answer,
she turns to her companions. 'Girls, girls!
We've got a birthday boy here.'

They let out a cheer and she turns back
and asks me, 'What's your name, sweetie?'

Daisy answers for me, 'It's Michael.'
The nuns begin to sing, 'Happy Birthday',
and the whole carriage of merrymakers
and plain-clothed home-goers all join in,
including Mum and Anna, who is now very
awake.

'So, how old are you sweetie?' our nun asks.
'I'm seventeen,' I reply.

'And how about your girlfriend?'
'She's not—' I begin.

'—I'm sixteen,' Daisy cuts in.
'Baker Street. Everyone out,' shouts another
one of the nuns.

'Goodnight, kids,' says my nun. Then
she leans into me and whispers: 'I think she
likes you.'

Christmas Day it's me, Mum and Anna,
but Mum's made a lot for just three of us.

She's done a nut roast and a turkey
with roast potatoes and vegetables.
There's vegan stuffing, normal stuffing,
pigs-in-blankets, vegan cocktail sausages,
there's vegan gravy and normal gravy.

'You've made too much, Mummy,' I say.

'That's good. Then Daisy can have some
when she comes tomorrow.'

I haven't invited Daisy round tomorrow
but she's come round on Boxing Day
for the past four years so Mum's assumption
makes sense. I've started to feel like
there's something between Daisy and me.

An obstacle.

I don't think I fancy her, I don't
think she fancies me – but there's something.

In the middle of dinner,
Mum bolts up
and across the dining room.
She grabs the house phone,
which we never use. She dials
and hands it to me. I tut
and mouth, 'Who is it?' to Mum.

I hear his voice: '*Naí?*',
which means 'Yes' in Greek.

'Merry Christmas, Grandad.'
I smile at Mum.

'*Kalá Christoúgenna*, Michalis,'
he replies.

Grandad asks me,
'Are you studying hard?'

'Yes, Grandad,' I say.

Then he asks,
'How's your girlfriend, Daisy?'

'She's not my girlfriend, Grandad.'
I laugh.

After dinner, Anna calls Trevor.

I call Uncle B,
who is just ten minutes
down the road
with Granny
and the Brown family.

He gets the whole family
to shout, 'Merry Christmas, Mikey!'

I hear Granny take hold
of the phone. 'Mikey, darling,
yuh uncle say
nex year he gon pay
fi us all to go Jamaica
fi Christmas.
Yuh muss cum wid us.'

People Like Me

I'd love to go to Jamaica
with Granny, Uncle B, Aunty B
and the rest of the family

but I've looked it up
and you can go to prison
for having gay sex there.

I'm old enough here,
why would my equal
rights not travel with me?

It's doesn't seem fair
for people like me in Jamaica,
to hide, to live in fear.

Conversation with Myself

I'm eighteen now. An adult. I feel like
I should know what I'm doing.
Like, do I really want to go to university?
I weigh up my options in my head.

Maybe I could get a job? *Doing what?*
I could take a gap year? *With what money?*
I could ask Uncle B for money? *No, it's time to be your own man.*

I could go to drama school?
You're not talented enough.
I could do a vocational course?
As if you can do anything practical.

Maybe I could publish a book?
Who would want to read that?
I guess university makes sense.
Yes, university makes sense.

Reasons to Go to University

Moving to a new city,
Brighton, the gay capital of the UK
and meeting gay guys my age.
Making new friends.
A chance to be a new me,
not having to hide
anything from anyone
– what I'm doing
and who I'm doing it with.
Living on campus
and having an en-suite bathroom.
African Caribbean Society.
LGBT Society.
Open mic night. A reason to write.

I'm put in a group with Rowan
for my A level drama performance.
Our teacher suggests
the play *Beautiful Thing.*

It's annoying that Faith
and Destiny are in our group, too.
I've been lucky to go through school
without any classes with them.
But they had to go and pick drama
for A level, didn't they?

They stopped being mean
when Grace got excluded
last year but they never apologised.
I can't say I forgive them
but I want a good grade for drama,
so decide to take charge.

I say, 'You're gonna be amazing
in this; I've watched the movie so many times.
I know exactly who everyone should play.
Faith, you'll play Sandra, the mum.
Destiny, you should play Leah, she's a singer.
Ben, you'll be Tony, he's Sandra's boyfriend.'
Ben winks at Faith and Destiny laughs.

I know Rowan would suit Tony more
but Ben has the biggest crush on Faith
and I still have a little crush on Rowan.
'Rowan, you'll be Ste, and I'll play Jamie.'

This means two things.
One: I get to give Rowan a massage.
Two: I get to kiss Rowan.

I tell Daisy at lunchtime:
'My day has arrived – I'm gonna kiss Rowan
in the play.'

She rolls her eyes. 'It's just acting –
he's still got a girlfriend, you know?'

I don't appreciate her
saying any of this when
I'm *this* excited for a kiss.

In rehearsal, we play out the massage
but agree to save the kiss
for the real performance.

I think of nothing else for weeks.
In a way, it's more pressure
to have this big build-up to the day.

After a rehearsal, Faith and Destiny come over.
'Michael, can we have a word with you,
please?' Faith says. Destiny looks serious.

Ben and Rowan are leaving, Rowan
turns back and waits by the door.
Faith notices me smiling at Rowan
over her shoulder and says sternly, 'In private.'

'Sorryyy!' Rowan says.

'What's this about?' I say, annoyed I can't
leave with Rowan, and ready
for an argument about the roles I assigned
them in the cast.

'Destiny and I wanted to say sorry
about how mean we were in Year 8.'

'And Year 9. And Year 10,' I say,
with a smile. *I can't believe they are
apologising. Am I imagining it?*

Destiny speaks. 'We're sorry for it all.'

'What exactly are you sorry for?' I ask.

'The little comments,' says Destiny.
'The dirty looks and' – she gets choked up –
'the notes in your bag.' She starts crying.

Faith puts an arm around her.

'I'm okay,' says Destiny,
smoothing down her hair.

If this is an act,
I wish she was this good
in our rehearsals.

'Someone in my family came out to me
recently and I've realised…' continues Destiny.
She looks to Faith to finish her sentence.
'We've realised…'

'We were complete bitches,' says Faith,
'and we feel so bad and so awkward
doing this play with you without knowing
if you hate us? Can you forgive us?'

'If we get an A, I'll forgive you.' I wink.

After our dress rehearsal,
Rowan says, 'It's been special
doing this play with you.
The other three are great but
you know how our scenes together
are just so intimate, it almost
feels like I'm really falling for you.'

I could have broken that line
in so many ways. Take what I want
from it. I could have latched on to
'feels like I'm really falling for you'
or 'I'm really falling for you'.
But 'almost' makes it all untrue.

The following day, when we do
the performance and finally kiss,
I'm thinking what Daisy said –
'It's just acting' – and I don't even
remember the touch of his lips on mine.

After the performance,
I notice Kieran is in the audience.
Did he come to see me?

No. He goes over to hug Faith
and Destiny. Who I have forgiven
already, regardless of what grade
we get.

Daisy comes over to me: 'Well done!
You were amazing!' she says loudly
and then she whispers, 'So, how did it feel
to kiss Rowan?'

'It's weird but I, like, didn't feel anything,'
I say, looking over at Kieran, who is laughing,
with his arm around Destiny's shoulder.

'Daisy, will you come to a gay club with me
sometime?'

'Of course. I thought you'd never ask.'
She laughs, puts her arm around my waist.
'Once exams are over, obviously.'

I call Granny B
to tell her my A level results.

She screams, 'Well don, darling!
Yuh muss tell yuh fada. I'm guh fi guh get him.'

She shouts his name three times.

A pause and then faintly, 'What is it?'
'It's Mikey pon de phone.'

A pause and fainter still, 'Tell him I'm busy.'

ROWAN: How did you do?

MICHAEL: I got an A for drama

ROWAN: That's great!
Everyone in our group got an A
We should all celebrate

MICHAEL: Sounds good. 👍
Message in the group chat?

Rowan changes the name of the group chat
from 'Beautiful Thing' to 'The A Team'
and changes the image
from the *Beautiful Thing* movie poster
to a picture of a black man
with a mohawk and lots of gold jewellery.

FAITH: Who's that man?

ROWAN: Mr T

FAITH: ??

ROWAN: From The A Team

DESTINY: I thought we were the A Team

MICHAEL: Yh
Because we all got A for drama?

FAITH: I'm so confused

BEN: I just looked up The A Team on YouTube 👍

ROWAN: 👍

DESTINY: ••

ROWAN: Nando's this Sunday?

DESTINY: I'm vegan

BEN: Since when?

DESTINY: It's been two weeks. I want to go to university as a better person

BEN: You should go to uni as Mr T

ROWAN:

DESTINY: How about the fair on the common?

MICHAEL: Yes!!!

ROWAN: Sounds good to me. Only if we can get churros

FAITH:

ROWAN: 6pm?

DESTINY: 👍

MICHAEL: 👍

ROWAN: Ben?

BEN: Cool

MICHAEL: I'm bringing Daisy. She's staying at mine this weekend

BEN: 'I pity the fool!' 😄

ROWAN: 😋

FAITH: 😄

Sunday evening,
Outside the House of Mirrors,
Ben holds Faith by the waist,
they are kissing.

Destiny is showing Rowan something
on her phone.

'What's that?' I ask Destiny.
'The video that turned me
and my brother vegan,' she says,
pretending to throw up.

'Where's Daisy?' Rowan asks. I shrug.
'I don't know. We're not talking.'

Rowan steps closer and puts his arm
around me. 'I'm sorry to hear that, man.
What happened?'

I take Rowan by the hand. 'Let's go
on some rides. In here!'

I pull him into
the House of Mirrors.

'Don't you wanna talk about Daisy?' he asks.
'Nah, I really don't,' I say, in front of a mirror
that makes my legs look really long
but my torso tiny.

'Okay, tell me something else then,'
says Rowan. His mirror makes his head
look massive. 'Do you still fancy me?'
He joins me at my mirror, which becomes
our mirror.

If I turned to him would he kiss me?

'I fancy that guy more.' I laugh, poke him
in the ribs and point to his reflection. I can't
make out his expression in the topsy-turvy
mirror.

THE PREVIOUS NIGHT

Saturday night, Daisy and I
go to our first club: G-A-Y.

I've been eighteen for nine months
but I didn't want to go without
my best friend. Daisy only
turned eighteen last week.

Daisy's wearing the red dress
that she didn't get to wear
to the Year 9 school disco.

We're waiting in line and she says,
'You have to protect me,
if any girls try to chat me up.
Tell them that we're together.'

'Daisy, the point of us being here
is for me to meet a guy.
How will that happen if we
pretend to be a couple?'

'I just don't want anyone thinking
I'm a lesbian,' she replies.

'What would be so wrong with that?' I ask.

'It makes me feel sick,
the idea of two women sleeping together.
Two men doesn't bother me
but two women, I don't get it.'

'What about it makes you feel sick?'
I ask through gritted teeth.

'I don't want to talk about it.
Will you just protect me from
any lesbians that try it on?'

'*They* need protecting from *you*.
You're a homophobe, Daisy.'

'Michael, you can't force me
to be comfortable with all this.
I'm not homophobic, I'm your best friend.
Nothing changed between us
when *you* came out in **B24**.'

'Well, school's over and **B24**
doesn't mean anything now.
I don't need an ignorant *best friend*.
Why don't you just go home.'

'My stuff is at your house; I was meant to be
staying the night, remember?'

'Fine, let's go back to mine.'

When we get home my mum is watching
Game of Thrones. 'You two are back early.'

I say the line I have been rehearsing
in my head, as we travelled home in silence.

'Daisy's not feeling well, she's just gonna
get her stuff and call her dad to pick her up.'

I can see from the way Mum squints
at me and smiles with a closed mouth at Daisy,
she knows something isn't right but she
simply says, 'Okay. I hope you feel better,
Daisy,' as she unpauses her programme.

Keeping out of our real drama and going
back to a world of fantasy.

House of Mirrors

Your best friend is a mirror.
Other friends ask after you
when you are standing right there.
'Where are you?' they ask.
'Why are you without your other self?'
You two are the ingredients
to make something brand new.
You cannot unbake a cake.
You can only slice. A knife is a mirror.
A best friend can be a knife.

A best friend can be a knife.
You can only slice. A knife is a mirror.
You cannot unbake a cake
to make something brand new.
You two are the ingredients.
'Why are you without your other self?'
'Where are you?' they ask,
when you are standing right there.
Other friends ask after you.
Your best friend is a mirror.

UNIVERSITY

Uncle B drives me
and my stuff to university.
He tells me how proud he is,
asks what I'm excited about
and what I'm nervous about.
I don't tell him I'm excited
and nervous about meeting guys,
having sex, maybe a relationship.
I tell him I'm excited to have
my freedom.

We're five minutes from
our destination
according to his sat nav,
and we hear sirens
and see flashing lights.
It's the police behind us.
My uncle pulls over,
I think, at first, to let them pass,
but I soon realise that
they are pulling *us* over.

They ask my uncle
if this is his car, to see his licence,
where are we going.
They tell him it's a very nice car,
ask him what he does for a living.

My usually polite uncle
is abrupt with the police,
asks them what business
they have stopping him.
Was he speeding?
Was there a problem
with one of his lights?
Did he fit the description
of a suspect they're looking for?

The police
say we can be on our way
and to have a nice day.
They get back in their car
and drive away.
'Are you okay?' I ask.

Uncle B begins:
'There's always something.
No matter how hard you work.
No matter how well you do.
How successful or respectable.
There's always something
that will remind you
you shouldn't get too comfortable.

I always thought education
and money was going
to earn me respect,
but a successful black man
is a threat. Pulling me over
for driving a nice car.
This isn't what I wanted
for your moving day
but this is what it's like
to be black in this country
or anywhere in the world.
They interrupt our joy.
Our history. Our progress.
They know they can't
stop us unless they kill us
but they can't kill us all,
so you're living your life
and suddenly interrupted
by white fear or suspicion.
They fear sharing anything.
Our success is a threat.'

I've never heard my uncle
speak in these terms, of them
and *us*. I've never thought
in these terms.   Until today.

Everything is here on campus,
everything I could need,
all of my lessons, the library,
shops, cafés, four bars
and my room, which isn't cheap:
I chose an en-suite
in the newest accommodation.
I figure if I'm taking out a loan
anyway, why not live it up?

Once we're all moved in,
I don't see much of my flatmates.
Since we all have our own
bathroom and no one has
any food in the kitchen but me.

There are four of them:
Kerry, Kevin, Luke and Sam,
who introduces herself as
Samantha and then says,
'But you can call me Sam.'

I introduce myself as Mike.
Mike feels right for this new chapter.
Michael is what Mum calls me.
Mikey is for Granny and Uncle B.
Mike is the man I am at university.

This will be my first
meal without Mum supervising.
My flatmate Kevin hovers
around the kitchen.
I'm making ackee and salt fish,
rice and peas
and baked plantain.
There's space for Kevin
if he wants to cook, too.
Not that he has any food.
I'm only using two hobs
and one shelf in the oven.
'Smells good, Mike.'

'It's ackee and salt fish,'
I say, offering a wooden spoonful.
He takes a tiny taste.
'So what is ackee?'
'It's a fruit,' I tell him.
'It comes in a tin.'
I fish the empty tin
out of our recycling bin.
I hand it to him and
take back the spoon.
'How fascinating,' he says,
examining it like an alien artefact.

I don't last long at Freshers' Fair
in Library Square. There are sports teams
in their full kits trying to sign people up.
The football, rugby and basketball teams
all look terrifying to me.

There are other groups of people at tables
with banners and flags, giving out their flyers.
I see a rainbow flag but I've already checked
on the Students' Union website to find out
when LGBT Society meets, so I don't go over.
I already have a reminder in my phone for it,
along with African Caribbean Society and
open mic night.

Instead, I go to a less intimidating table
of posters: there's one with a black cat
and French writing, another of clocks that look
like they're melting; there's one of a big blue
and white wave; there's a *Pulp Fiction* movie
still of Samuel L. Jackson and John Travolta
pointing their guns; there's the *Trainspotting*
'Choose Life' monologue. I decide to buy one
of Audrey Hepburn in *Breakfast at Tiffany's*.
I haven't seen the movie but I love her
long black gloves and her long black dress.

I put Audrey up on my new bedroom wall,
next to Beyoncé and Bob Marley from home.

Apart from these three posters there's not
much to say about the person who lives here – a row of
footwear: dirty white Converse,
bright white Adidas, black Nikes.

My clothes in the drawers are navy and light
blue jeans, a grey tracksuit, black and white
tees, Calvin Klein boxers Mum bought from
TK Maxx and socks Mum also bought, from
Primark.

My books: the reading for the first term
of my English degree, some favourites
from school, *The Complete Works of
William Shakespeare* and some poetry
that Mum bought me: Maya Angelou,
Gil Scott-Heron and Benjamin Zephaniah.

Freshers' Week is two entire
weeks of, 'What's your name?'
'What do you study?'
'Where are you from?'

If you don't find any common
ground in these three questions
people move on.

The big three:
I'm Mike. I'm doing English.
I'm from London.

Some, without any prompting,
start talking about their gap year;
how they went to Asia or Africa,
backpacking or volunteering.

I've come straight from school
and I've not been anywhere but Cyprus
to visit Mum's family.

I go to the African Caribbean Society.
Most of them are Londoners like me,
but some are international students
from African and Caribbean countries,
some African-American and Canadian,
but Londoners are the biggest group.

People talk about being from South
or East London, like that matters here.
'A room of black kids gathered together
and our only similarity is being black,'
I say to Nana, a British-Ghanian girl
from South I just met ten minutes ago.

'But you're not black, you're mixed,'
says Nana. 'No offence, Mike, but
you said you're Jamaican and Greek.'
'Greek-Cypriot,' I calmly correct her.
'What I mean is: I heard there's a Greek
Society here. You could go there, too.'

The Hellenic Society caters
for Greek and Greek-Cypriot students.
I take a moment at the open door,
looking timidly around the room.
A guy approaches, greets me in
Greek: '*Geia sou. Xereis na milas ellinika?*'

'Hello. No, I don't speak Greek.'
Responding to the question, which
I understand, but don't feel confident
enough to reply to in my mother's tongue.

Outside Mum's family
I have never felt Cypriot enough.
I remember back to Cyprus and how I even
felt like an outsider within my own family.

'I'm Christos, it's good to meet you,'
he says, reaching out an open hand.
He wears a plain white T-shirt and light
blue jeans.

'I'm Mike or Michalis,' I reply,
embarrassed by my lack of language
and how handsome he is.

His hair is almost black and so is his
thick beard; his eyebrows nearly meet.
His eyes are so dark I can see myself
in them. His firm grip and eye contact
remain. 'Michalis,' he says, with a wink.
'A good Greek name.'

Someone calls him away: '*Éla*, Christo.'
He politely excuses himself, leaving me
alone again. I slip away, unnoticed.

I Want to Be a Pink Flamingo

Pink. Definitely pink.
I want my feathers to match
the hue you imagine.
I want to blend in.
Nothing but flamingoness.

David Attenborough would say,
'Here we see the most typical flamingo.'

Though I don't want to be the most,
just typical. A wrapping-paper pattern.
I don't want to stand apart.
Nothing different about my parts.
My beak just a beak, my head just a head.
My neck, body, wings. Simply fit for purpose.
Standing on one leg, just like the rest.
Pink. Definitely pink.

I go to the LGBT Society.
We sit in a circle and go round
saying our names and pronouns:
he/him, she/her, they/them.

How do you want other people
to refer to you?

A trans man called Seth,
with the pronouns he/him,
says he wishes his trans identity
wasn't questioned
with regards to his body.
'I wish people would understand,
some men have vaginas.'

My turn: 'I'm Mike, he/him.'

Some Men Have Vaginas

He said he was a gay man
with a vagina and I, penis heavy
and light of foot, wondered
if gay meant the same to him
as it did to me, wondered
if man was in mind or body.
Because I wear my man,
strip down bare to my man.
In the mirror, there, I am.
For me, man has merely been
a matter of circumstance,
not a journey or discovery.
I rarely had to fight for it,
rarely want to fight against it,
never wanted to shed skin
to reveal somebody else.
I never questioned it until
he said, 'Some men have vaginas.'
I understood it to be true
but it left me feeling nothing

more than a tool, who knew
nothing about being a man
outside his own body.

I feel like Goldilocks:
trying to find a group of people
the perfect fit for me.
A group that's 'just right'.
I didn't feel black enough
for African Caribbean Society,
I didn't feel Greek enough
for Hellenic Society,
I didn't feel queer enough
for LGBT Society
But I've got to find a group
that's just right for me.

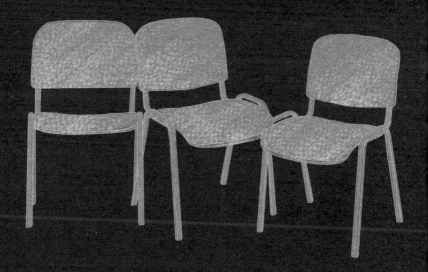

I know I have to go
when I see the poster
on the notice board
in the Students' Union.

DRAG SOCIETY
in capital letters
with a date and time
and a room number.

Why have I not noticed
this poster before now?

There's a photo of a group
of people of many shapes,
colours and gender expressions
in costume and make-up.

I make up my mind,

I'm going to do that,

whatever that is,

whatever that means.

DRAG

I've seen *Kinky Boots*
and *RuPaul's Drag Race*.
In A level drama
we were told DRAG
stands for Dressed
Resembling A Girl.
It happened in theatre
in original stagings
of plays by Shakespeare.
Women were not
allowed to perform.
Young men would play
the female roles.

No one is in costume but a forthcoming
performance is the reason we're all here.
Drag Society feels different from any other
Students' Union society I've been to so far.

If you didn't know why we were here,
you couldn't tell what brought us together.
No one person looks similar to the other.
We're not just here because we're 'queer';
we're here to create a show together
but first we must get to know each other.

'Here at Drag Soc,' begins the president,
'we use our drag names and pronouns
of our drag character. I'm Mzz Behaviour,
em-zed-zed. You can call me Mzz B and
my pronouns are "they" and "them".'

I'm still getting used to they/them pronouns,
but they/them makes sense for Mzz B.

They are both handsome and beautiful.
They have faint stubble showing
under their light application of make-up,
mahogany foundation, purple eye shadow
and pink lips that match their outfit.

Their outfit reminds me of the Chanel suit
that Marge Simpson buys and then
feels really guilty about. Their hair is not blue
or Marge Simpson high but a perfect
round afro. Mzz B is already an icon to me.

Mzz B catches me staring at them
several times as everyone is introducing
their drag persona, one by one around
the circle, with names and pronouns.

I'm not confused; I'm just an overly
curious person. So when they say
the name and pronoun for their drag
characters, I want to ask: *What's your real
name? What's your real gender?*

But what would my agenda be
if I were to ask those questions?

And what name can't be changed?

I changed my surname at seven.
Now nineteen, I'm being asked to create
a new identity for a different purpose:
a stage name.

Just like Onika Tanya Maraj
became
Nicki Minaj

and Stefani Joanne Angelina Germanotta
became
Lady Gaga.

But Madonna, Beyoncé and RuPaul
didn't need new names: they simply dropped
their surnames, left them backstage
in the wings with their family and friends.

It's my turn. I don't know what to say.

I can't explain what brought me here today
apart from that poster; I don't know
if the people on the poster are the same people
here in this room, no one is in costume.

I don't want to assume, I feel too shy to ask,
but when I saw that poster I simply knew
that Drag Soc was something I had to do.

I didn't realise I would need to decide
my character as I stepped through the door.

Only one name comes to mind. It's like
I've said it before: 'I am The Black Flamingo
and my pronouns are he and him,' I declare.
I'm sure of this for the first time ever.

They look at each other, then at me.

Then Mzz B asks, 'So are you a king,
a queen or…?'

'Neither,' I say. 'I'm just a man and I want
to wear a dress and make-up on stage.
I want to know how it feels to publicly
express a side of me I've only felt privately
when playing with my Barbie as a boy.
It was only at home that I'd play with that toy;
I knew Mum loved me more than
anyone else and with her I could be myself.
I didn't think boys could do ballet, certainly
not a black boy and definitely not me.
I was already suspicious that people were
nice to me despite me being different.
I never wanted to take my difference too far.'

I continue,
'Before I came here
I didn't want to wear a dress,
I didn't want to be that stereotype.

I know that's wrong,
my thinking was wrong,
the different ones
are often the most strong.

I know trans
and gender nonconforming people
started our movements,
won our freedoms.

I'm a man
and I want to be a free one.

I'm a man
and I want to put a dress on.'

Mzz B says,
'Great monologue!
Keep that.
You can use it in your act.'

I feel safe in this room
with my new drag family;
I carry this room with me
for the rest of the week.
This room has many other
functions to other people,
just another room in the
Students' Union building,
but when we meet here,
it's a place without fear.

Campus is full of white
guys with locs.
There's something about it
that doesn't feel right.

There's something about it
that makes my locs not
feel right either,
even though I'm not white.

I don't really know
what this hairstyle means
but it looks good on me,
shoulder-length and neat;
most white locs look a mess,
strands of straight hair
sticking out everywhere
and their roots coming undone.
I tend to my roots daily,
twist them with beeswax
to ensure they endure
wind, rain and the shower.
I wash them weekly,
tighten them neatly
so they grow strong –
but do they belong?

It happens on campus
and when I go into the city.
Black people notice me.
We nod to acknowledge
each other, and sometimes
we smile. It's odd to me
coming from London.

It's a nod that says, 'I know
we are small in numbers
but we are watching over
each other.' It's a smile
that says, 'We don't have
to know each other to
show each other love.'

It's a nod I get in London
but only from Rastafarians
who'd assume I am part
of their religion, but here
in Brighton locs is a hairstyle
with different connotations.

For weeks we are
in the same English lectures
and don't speak.
At most we nod
if our eyes meet
elsewhere on campus.
In the Students' Union bar,
when a mutual acquaintance
doesn't introduce us,
we do it ourselves.
She is astonished
we don't know each other.
The only two
black men on a course
of over two hundred!

Lennie looks fully black,
not mixed like me.
He is only a little bit taller
than me but he's stocky –
I can't tell if it's muscle or fat
because he wears a baggy
black Nike tracksuit.
He has locs like me
but longer and thicker.
Lennie looks strong.

After our lecture the next day,
we walk together and
I say, whilst passing the spliff,
'I didn't want to speak to you
just because we're both black with locs.'

I say, 'I don't like white people
to know I smoke weed –
they assume I'm a dealer.'

Lennie says, 'I only smoke weed
for my chronic back pain.'

I applaud
his clever use
of the Dr Dre reference.

He doesn't know it.

I say, 'How can you not know Dr Dre?'

Lennie replies, laughing,
'Why aren't you a drug dealer?'

Lennie and I laugh about white people
always trying to touch our hair.
'What baffles me,' I say, 'is when they ask
but their hand is already there.'

He adds, 'Or when you tell them *No*
and they get so offended about it.'
'*Exactly!*' I say. 'They feel entitled
to touch us just because they were gracious
enough to ask.'

'That's just their general entitlement
and privilege,' says Lennie.
My flatmate Kerry appears:
'Am I interrupting the Black Panther meeting?'

And I'm not sure if she means the revolutionary
organisation or the Marvel superhero.
Lennie seems to see I feel awkward;
he defuses the situation: 'Did you know
that a black panther is not actually a species?
It's a melanin variant of any big cat.
In Asia and Africa they are leopards,
and in America they are jaguars.'

I give Lennie the Wakanda salute.
He raises a fist to give the Black Power salute.

Kerry giggles, uncomfortably.
'Are you walking towards our flat?'

'Yeah, but I'm just talking to Lennie.'

'Oh, okay,' she says, 'I'll see you later.'
She speeds off ahead of us.

Lennie asks me, 'If you could have
any superpower, what would it be?

I joke, 'To be invisible to white people.'

Lennie:
'But then your mum couldn't see you.'

'Sometimes I'm not sure she does,'
I say, and I don't know if I'm still joking.

My phone buzzes.
I pass the spliff back to Lennie.
It's my calendar, a reminder for
'Open mic night'. Tonight!

I haven't arranged to go with anyone.
'Lennie, have you got plans tonight?'

'Are you asking me on a date?' Lennie says,
with a mischievous smile.

I pause. Thinking if I did ask him on a date,
would he be interested? Would I be
interested in dating Lennie? 'No.
I want to go to open mic night tonight.'

'That sounds awful.' Lennie laughs.
'I'd rather smoke on my own
and listen to quality music, not awful covers
and wannabe singer-songwriters.'

'There's poetry, too!' I say enthusiastically.
'Stop! You're making it worse,' laughs Lennie,
passing the spliff back to me. 'Mikey boy,
you're on your own.'

I decide I like how Lennie's chosen
to call me Mikey.

I arrive just in time
to sign up for the last of twelve open mic slots.
The night is exactly what Lennie said
it would be. The Students' Union bar
is usually so busy, but it seems people have
avoided it tonight.

It's mostly just the performers;
only some of them have a companion.

The host looks like a rock star –
black leather jacket, skinny jeans, long hair.
He can't sing but he 'warms us up'
with three songs on his guitar before
the open mic begins.

Out of twelve of us, the only other 'poet'
is a white guy with locs called Vegan Warrior,
and his poem compares eating meat
to the Transatlantic slave trade. It's terrible.

I don't pay much attention to the singers,
partly because I'm nervous, partly because
they're not very good, and partly jealously
that I don't sing any more.

It's my turn. I step up to the mic and read:

I Come From

I come from shepherd's pie and Sunday
roast, jerk chicken and stuffed vine leaves.
I come from travelling through taste buds
but loving where I live. I come from
a home that some would call broken.

I come from DIY that never got done.
I come from waiting by the phone
for him to call. I come from waving
the white flag to loneliness. I come from
the rainbow flag and the Union Jack.

I come from a British passport
and an ever-ready suitcase. I come from
jet fuel and fresh coconut water.
I come from crossing oceans
to find myself. I come from deep issues
and shallow solutions.

I come from a limited vocabulary
but an unrestricted imagination.
I come from a decent education
and a marvellous mother.

I come from being given permission
to dream but choosing to wake up
instead. I come from wherever I lay
my head. I come from unanswered
questions and unread books, unnoticed
effort and undelivered apologies
and thanks. I come from who I trust
and who I have left.

I come from last year and last year
and I don't notice how I've changed.
I come from looking in the mirror
and looking online to find myself.
I come from stories, myths, legends
and folk tales. I come from lullabies
and pop songs, hip-hop and poetry.

I come from griots, grandmothers
and her-story tellers. I come from
published words and strangers' smiles.
I come from my own pen but I see
people torn apart like paper, each a story
or poem that never made it into a book.

After the open mic,
I'm talking to this couple.
Simon is white;
Mia might not be.
Simon is studying engineering;
Mia is doing media.

'I would love to film one of your poems.'
Mia says enthusiastically. 'Do you have
a YouTube channel or an Instagram?'

Before I can answer, I see him
approaching, behind her. White,
blond like Simon, six foot something,
pecs at my eye-line, biceps bulging
and what a smile! I don't understand
why he's wearing a vest in autumn
but I'm not complaining. *His arms are to die for!*

'Madame. Monsieur.' He hands
a glass of white wine to Mia
and a pint of Guinness to Simon.

'Hi. I'm Mike,' I say. I mean: *Who are you?*
'Hey, Mike, Jack. Great poetry,'
he continues, 'or is it spoken word?'
He puts his huge hand on my shoulder.

Mia looks at Jack's hand, then
says to Simon, 'I fancy a rollie.
Have you got your baccy, babe?'

'Yeah,' says Simon to Mia, then
he turns to Jack. 'We'll be right back.'

I ask Jack if he wants a drink.
He says, 'I don't drink any more.'
So I don't get a drink either.

We sit at a quiet corner table.
We chat at first about the false divide
between poetry and spoken word,
and then about how he wishes he could
write poetry and I try to convince him
that he can if he wants to. I'll help him,
if he wants me to—?

Then he tells me he doesn't study here.
He's Simon's brother, just visiting.
He says he loves visiting Simon
because: 'Everyone here is so free.
Back in our town, people are restricted
by family expectations and childhood
reputations.'

'I wasn't made for university,' says Jack.
'I'm a practical person. I make a good
living in construction. And I get to travel
with it sometimes. I'm always surrounded
by men and their banter and their anger
and their hurt, and sometimes I just want
to hug them, you know, invite them to open up.'

I do know, Jack. I really do. I'm following
his monologue but all I can think about
is how much I want to stop him mid-sentence
with a kiss.

But Jack continues:
'I'm not gay but, men, we can understand
each other and yet we never talk honestly.
We put it all on our girlfriends –
not that I have one. I've read about this
online, it's work for them, emotional labour.'

I'm hearing this semi-coherent account
from this man in touch with something
that many men will never figure out, but
one phrase he said is stuck in my head.

'I'm not gay'

'I'm not gay but'

'but'

'but, men'

'men'

'men, we can understand each other.'

I know before I say it, why I'm saying it.
Because I feel there's a connection.
Why did he say he doesn't have a girlfriend?
Why has he been talking to me for so long?

'But you're not straight, are you?' I blurt out,
interrupting him, but not with a kiss.

He stops speaking, then opens his mouth,
closes it, looks to the floor, then back to me.

Can he see my longing? My curiosity?
Can he feel the connection or have I
constructed something out of nothing?

'Mike, you're a beautiful man, interesting
and talented too; I'm enjoying talking to you.'

I smile until I realise he's deflected
the question with compliments and before
either one of us can say any more,
Simon reappears. 'Oh good, you're still here.
We're heading back. Are you coming, Jack?'

And that's the only question he needs to
answer. Here is his escape route without
causing any offence. And I prepare myself
to say goodbye, possibly for ever and

the pause

goes on for too long and Simon says, with
a laugh in his smile, 'Sorry, did I interrupt?'

'You go ahead. I'll be all right, with Mike.'

I'm walking across campus
back to my room with Jack
in silence, not quite comfortable,
not quite awkward.

I want to know what Jack's thinking.
I look up at him. He looks down
at me and smiles and I smile back.

I look forward.

Just keep walking.
Nearly there now.

'So, this is my room,' I say,
gesturing around randomly.
'I have an en-suite bathroom,'
I say with unwarranted pride.
I point to the bed. 'Shall we?'
I just mean: Shall we sit?

I realise too late what's implied
is something else entirely
and it's not what I meant
but it's definitely what I want.
I want it to be with him.
I'm ready to lose my virginity.

'Lose' doesn't sound right.
This won't be an accident.

How else can I say it? I'm ready
to give him my virginity?

'Give' doesn't sound right.
I don't see it as a gift to him.

We're sitting on my bed now.
He kicks off his Reebok Classics.
I untie the laces of my Converse
and pull them off.

I don't think he's a virgin.
We don't say anything at first.

I turn to face him,
he turns towards me.

I ask him, 'Can I kiss you?'
and he says, 'Yes.'

I ask him, 'Can I touch you?'
and he says, 'Yes.'

I ask him, 'Will you use a condom?'
and he says, 'Yes.'

I ask him, 'Will you stay the night?'
and he says, 'Yes.'

He falls asleep before me
and I lie wide awake, thinking
this is how it should be.
Meeting someone in real life,
not online or on an app.
Meeting someone randomly,
not just in a gay bar – in any bar.
Or anywhere – at a bus stop,
a shop, walking down the street,
how other people get to meet.

He falls asleep beside me
and I get to look at him,
really look at him; he's so
classically attractive, it's unreal,
like a statue of Perseus
or Michelangelo's David,
somewhat cliché
and not once did I think,
He'd never be into me
and not once did I think,
He's got to be straight.

He's sleeping next to me;
we just had sex, he's not straight.
I don't think I turned him
gay or bi. I invited him to see
a possibility and he accepted.

In the morning, I put my hand on his solid
chest and my head on his shoulder.

We stay like this for just a few seconds
before he gets up and starts to get dressed.

'Are you okay?' I ask
and he says, 'Yes.'

'Are you sure?' I ask
and he says, 'Yes.'

'Please talk to me,' I say.
He says, 'I'll message you later.'

'When will I see you again?' I ask.

After he leaves, I want to tell
someone, anyone, that I am
no longer a virgin. I'm nineteen
and no one I know is a virgin
or, maybe, like me, no one admits
to being a virgin. We let
people assume we have
experience by acting confident.

Whenever my phone buzzes
I check to see if it's from him

and if it's not, I put it down again.

I only met this guy last night
and now he's all I can think about.
He'll be heading back home,
two hundred miles away,
to his job in construction.

I take apart the night in my head.
Was there something I said
or did wrong? Were we wrong
to rush into sex? Should I have
left him wanting more until
the next time he came to visit
Simon?

Then I realise I don't know Jack
or Simon's surname and
we never swapped numbers.

When he left this morning
saying he would message me,
did he know he wasn't going to?

It feels like the one and only time
my mum slapped me. More shocking
than painful.

That evening, I go to the busy
Students' Union bar hoping to see Simon.
I'm there for three hours alone, slowly sipping
a rum and Coke, phone on the table,
Moleskine open on a blank page, Cross pen
refusing to speak. Until, finally:

Maybe I'm a Merman

Maybe I'm a merman.
No sea witch stole my song.
I decided to stop singing, to avoid
the attention it was bringing.

I have no home under the sea,
I've always lived on this land
but I look out as if there were
more for me beyond the shore.

I have not found the man
of my dreams, nor am I
the man I'm expected to be,
but maybe I'm a merman.

Maybe I have a tale to tell.
Maybe I have a spell to break.
My merman voice is broken.
My merman song is spoken.

I look up. I see Simon and Simon sees me.

He pauses before coming up to me. He says,
'My brother didn't give me a blow by blow
account but he told me enough and I figured
the rest out. I don't think it's the start
of something for you two, it was just one
of those things he needed to do.
I've known him all my life and he's not gay,
he just feels a lot of things. People would
always say he was different but it doesn't take
much to be different where we're from –
people took the piss out of me for reading
and coming to university. Where we're from
there's not much diversity and he's just full
of so much curiosity; whenever he comes
to visit me he sleeps with someone. Granted,
you're the first guy and I can see why you
caught his eye up on that stage, all confident
with your words and sense of self, speaking
and being heard. It's amazing what you do,
I applaud you and I'm sure, in the moment,
he adored you. You see, he's never had that,
we've never had that, but he's had you now,
Mike, and that's that.'

In my room alone,
I don't know who to reach out to.
It should be Daisy.

MICHAEL: Hey Daisy! I miss you. How's uni?

MICHAEL: Hey Rowan! How's drama school?

The next morning,
I wake up late for my lecture
so I decide to skip it.

I get the bus into town and go
to Brighton Beach with my notebook.

I have a missed call
from Mum but I don't want
to speak to her today.

My hair is being annoying
and blowing in my face,
so I tie it up, taking two locs
from the back at my neck
and wrapping them around
the rest and tie a bow.

Just breathe, I tell myself.
Just breathe.

On Brighton Beach

I let my breathing
    catch the timing
        of the waves;
    meditate.

    I don't swim,
        surf or paddle.
           I don't set foot
    in the water at all.

When
I need to breathe
    I sit
    on Brighton Beach.

I love to know
    I live on an island.
        I know my people
    are island people.

I am an island.
    Boy becoming a man.
        I am at university
discovering my identity.

    I see wide open sea
        stretch out before me,
            but I know the big city
    is where I'll return.

When I sit here
    on this beach I
        close my eyes,
    picture my position

    on the coastline;
        see the whole country,
            continents and planet,
    feel reassuringly small.

I remember the 'sandcastles'
Anna and I built
on our day trip to Brighton,
how she didn't care there were pebbles
and not sand
but how on the journey
I was so fearful
that she was going to cry
when we got there,
that she would only be happy
with sand
but she didn't mind
that her 'sandcastles'
didn't stay
in the shape of the bucket;
she was perfectly happy to play
with pebbles
and call it a sandcastle
anyway.

Men Are Sandcastles

Men are sandcastles made out of pebbles
and the bucket is patriarchy: if you remove it,
we fear we won't be able to hold ourselves
together, we pour in cement to fill the gaps
to make ourselves concrete constructions.

I'm surprised that it's all talk
in the next two meetings of Drag Society,
and no costumes or make-up tutorials.
Mzz B knows a lot about drag history,
American and British,
and the differences between them.
Mzz B is not keen on beauty queens
unless they have something to say.

'If all you want to do is look flawless,
that's valid, but you can do that at home
and post pictures on the Internet.
Why do you need to be on stage?
What do you want to say? Who are you?
What do you want from an audience?
What do you want to make them think?
How do you want to make them feel?
Do you want them to laugh? Cry? Get angry?
You've got to know. You've got to be
the one who's in control up there.
All I can do is introduce you and warm up
the audience but once you're
in that spotlight, it's yours to own.'

I see the heels from the window
and I am sure, as sure as I was
when I first saw the poster for
Drag Soc, these are the heels
for me: black with a lace pattern,
four inches, manageable I think.

I'm terrified of what the lady
in the shop will think when
I ask to try them on. Will they
even have them in my size?
'Size seven, yes, of course,'
she casually replies. 'Just these?'

They fit perfectly in the shop
but I didn't practise walking,
relieved no one made fun of me,
no one looked at me oddly.
I took them off and to the counter,
paid for them and left quickly.

Every evening in my room,
instead of socialising, I practise
walking in my new heels.
I play songs by Rihanna,
Nicki Minaj and Queen Bey,
try to channel fierce femininity.

I turn to my poster of Beyoncé
and blow her a kiss.

Mum calls me every day
to tell me she misses me,
ask me about my day
and tell me about her day.
Mostly, I have little to say
but she is never lost for words.
She complains about work
and Anna's latest antics,
elaborating on every story
with painstaking detail.
She never spoke to me
like this when I lived at home.
Absence makes her heart
grow more... communicative?

She says,
'Anna really misses you.
She sleeps in your bedroom.
Why don't you call her?
Are you coming home soon?
Maybe for your birthday?
Maybe we can visit you?'

'Not for my birthday,' I say.
'I have an essay I need to do
and I'm feeling the pressure.'

On the morning of my birthday,
Uncle B calls to say he'll take me shopping
when I'm next in London.

I don't tell him I'd rather see the stars.
I left my telescope at home in London,
handed it down to Anna.

Mum and Anna call; together
they sing 'Happy Birthday' to me.
Mum asks what I have planned today.

I say I don't have any plans; I have
too much work to do, so much reading,
and two essays due next week.
It's so much harder than A levels.

I miss Daisy and not just how she helped me
with my school work. She stood by me
when I came out and became
a part of my family. The one
I could speak to about Rowan and Kieran.

I didn't tell her everything,
but almost. And she wasn't my girlfriend,
but almost.

LENNIE: HBD! Want a birthday spliff later?

MICHAEL: I forgot I told you it was my birthday. I must've been high 😂

LENNIE: 😆

LENNIE: So?

MICHAEL: Thanks for remembering. I just want to ignore this day 😬

LENNIE: Want a non-birthday spliff instead?

MICHAEL: No
But thanks
I'll see you tomorrow

LENNIE:

I pause when Daisy's name
flashes on my phone screen.

I didn't expect to hear from her.
We haven't spoken since summer.

Why is Daisy calling me?
I guess to say, 'Happy birthday!'

And, yes, that's how she begins
and when I don't say anything,
she continues, 'I'm sorry.'

'What are you sorry for?' I ask.

'You know what for,' says Daisy.
'For what I said at the club.

I didn't realise how offensive
I was being. My girlfriend –
yes, I said girlfriend –
Chloe explained to me
it was because I was in denial
about my sexuality.

Chloe's amazing, I met her
on my first day here
and we've been inseparable
for the past six weeks

and yesterday I told her
about our argument.
I told her what I said, even
though I was embarrassed.
I think I needed to come out
to her about it, you know?
I already knew what I said
was awful. I'm sorry, Michael.
Chloe said that I said
what I said because of
internalised homophobia.
That I was homophobic
towards myself as well
as towards you. I think
that's what Chloe said.
Does that make sense?'

It does kind of make sense
and I'm relieved, in a way.
It turns out my homophobic
best friend is actually gay.

I tell Daisy, 'I'm glad you called,
we should speak again soon,
maybe meet up over Christmas.'

I don't tell her I'm lonely.
I just want to get off the phone.
It's making it worse.

I mostly keep to myself but for Halloween
my flatmates are having a party.
I've not told them it's my birthday but I join in.
We bring autumn leaves into our flat.
We make the most typical choices
of costume: a witch, a vampire, a werewolf.

I'm a ghost.

My costume is a white sheet
with two holes cut out for my eyes.
I guess it's more of a disguise.

No one who comes to the party knows
that it's my birthday. Most bring
their own booze and ask me who
I know here. I tell them I live here.

They say, 'Great party!' and offer me
one of their beers or a swig from
whatever spirit they are clutching.
I like being around people this way.
Somewhere I feel safe. I can retreat
to my room if I want to at any time.

After seven beers, I retreat to my room
and sit on my bed.

I imagine removing my white
sheet to reveal I am wearing a tutu
and ballet pointe shoes. I go en-pointe.
Everyone at the party begins to sing
'Happy Birthday'. Kieran appears holding
a cake with just one candle. I look closer
at the candle and it's not a candle.

It's Rowan, in miniature, his red hair standing
upright like a flickering flame. I make a wish as
I blow and Rowan disappears
and so does everyone else except for Kieran.

He says, 'Happy birthday, Michael.'

He leans in to kiss me and I close my eyes.
His lips feel light as a feather and I open
my eyes to find one black feather on my lips
and no Kieran and I cough and I cough
and I cough up black feather after black
feather.

I leave the house party
and decide to go to
Omen,
the gay club in town,
dumping my white sheet
in the dustbin on my way
to the bus stop.

I'm wearing my Converse,
navy blue Levi's jeans
and a light blue Levi's shirt.

I think a club is better than
an app. It's real life
and I can dance there.
The first thing I notice
when I get there: the outfits
are not like any Halloween
costumes I've seen before.

Lots of men have thick beards
and hairy chests. A topless DJ
with a smooth chest and chiselled abs
plays a pounding music
I don't recognise.

Most men look straight
through me or perhaps they don't
see me on the dance floor
when they bump into me.

No one says sorry.
No one speaks to me.
No one smiles at me.

Someone runs their fingers
through my hair. Startled,
I turn around to see him.
'I love your costume,' he says.

'Sorry?' I reply, forgetting
what I might look like
in this sea of white.
'That's a wig, isn't it?
Your costume, you're Bob Marley?'

Before my seminar the next day,
I tell Lennie about the club.

'What did you say to him?'
Lennie asks with a grin.

'I just walked away,' I reply.
'I'm sick of hearing it, Lennie.'

'But you do look a bit like him,
you have to admit.' Lennie tilts
his head to the side and raises
an eyebrow, then laughs.
'You should've invited me.
I could've been your wing-man.'

'Time for class, Mike,' says Sienna,
a girl in my seminar group,
as she floats past us
in a long, dark green dress
with tiny white polka dots;
with books under her arm,
she glides into the seminar room.
My eyes follow her in but my feet
stay grounded. When she's out of earshot,
Lennie exclaims, 'She's fit!'
I pretend I haven't noticed.

'Really? Come on, Mikey, you might be gay
but you're not blind,' says Lennie.

'You better get in there,' he continues.
He waves to Sienna, who is looking at us
from her seat and she waves back.
She brushes her long red hair off her shoulder,
leans forward with her chin in her hand.
I go in and take my seat next to her.

'Thank you for joining us, Mr Angeli,'
says our tutor, closing the door on Lennie.

LENNIE: You've got to introduce me to her

I hold my phone with both hands under
the table and turn my body so my back is
to Sienna and she can't see my screen.

MICHAEL: You can introduce yourself 🙄

LENNIE: Come on, Mikey. Be my wing-man. 🙏
Do you know if she's single?

MICHAEL:

LENNIE: Do some detective work

MICHAEL: Okay. I'll see what I can do

Our tutor asks: 'Mr Angeli, are we keeping you
from something more important?'

I didn't realise the seminar had started. I reply,
'No. Sorry.' I put my phone away.
Sienna is shaking her head at me but smiling.

At the end of the seminar,
Sienna turns to me.
'A group of us are going
to a club in town tonight.
Do you want to join us?'

'Who's going?' I ask her.

She lists six names, I don't know
any of them. But I see
my opportunity. 'Can I bring
my friend, Lennie?' I reply.

'The more the merrier,' says Sienna.

Later that evening, Lennie and I approach
Sienna at the bus stop. I'm still wearing
my blue jeans, white T-shirt and denim shirt
from earlier but Lennie has changed.

He is wearing a dark green Nike tracksuit.
Sienna is wearing a red jumpsuit and red
stilettos. Lennie's tracksuit would match what
Sienna was wearing earlier. I notice clothes
more since joining Drag Soc. Sienna's outfit
clashes with her hair.

I take a breath and prepare myself to be
introduced to more people, but Sienna
steps away from the crowd. 'Hey, boys!
The others have all bailed on me. It looks like
it's a threesome.'

'Oh, I thought those were your friends,' I say,
pointing to the people under the bus shelter.

'No,' says Sienna, 'it's just us. Tonight can be
about making new friends.' Sienna smiles at
Lennie and Lennie smiles at Sienna. I feel like
I should leave them to it.

When we get to the club,
they're playing Little Mix.
Sienna wants to dance but Lennie doesn't.

He says, 'You two go for it.
I'll get the drinks in. Rum and Coke?'

'Yes, please,' I say.

'Vodka lemonade for me,' says Sienna,
as she takes my hand and leads me
to the dance floor.

It's a rainbow sea of girls in jumpsuits.
I'm amazed at how well Sienna can dance
in heels; occasionally she puts her hands
on my shoulders to steady herself.
When she's close like this I study her
make-up, the flick of her black eyeliner,
the contouring on her cheek, her bright
red lips with a darker outline.

'I love your make-up!' I shout over the music.

'What did you say?' says Sienna.
If I can hear her why can't she hear me?

'Shall we go back to Lennie?' I point to him.

Later, in the smoking area,
while Lennie rolls us a spliff,
I tell Sienna what happened with Jack
and what Simon said to me.

'He sounds like a right idiot,' she says,
sympathetically squeezing my arm.

'Which one?' Lennie asks, handing
the finished spliff to Sienna.
I didn't think he was listening.

'The both of them, actually,' says Sienna,
and she takes just one toke
and passes the spliff to me.

There's a comfortable silence
as I take two tokes – one for Jack,
one for Simon.

I pass the spliff on to Lennie.
'I could never do it,' he says.
'I couldn't have sex with a guy,
no matter how drunk or high.'

I reply, 'You never know until you try.
Maybe I'm just that irresistible.'

Lennie chokes on a mouthful of smoke.
'If you were, Jack would've called you.'

He pulls no punches, says it straight.

He passes the spliff to Sienna,
who is trying hard not to laugh.

Sienna skips her turn
and passes it to me, asking,
'So, what's your type, Mike?'

I immediately say,
'Tall, white, big biceps
and a killer smile.'

I'm describing Jack
but Sienna and Lennie
haven't met him
so they don't know that.

I take a toke of the spliff.
'That's messed up,' says Lennie.
He looks serious.

'What is?' I say softly,
passing him the spliff.

'That she asked your type
and you said "white".'

I turn to Lennie and say,
'I don't know anyone
black and gay.'
And it's true, but it feels
like a cop out.

'I only date black guys,' says Sienna.

'That's messed up, too!' shouts Lennie.
'Do you two hear yourselves?'

'You both need to understand
the black woman, black man,
black trans person is always last
to be thought of as attractive
in this white supremacist society.
We are all – black and white alike
– shown a beauty standard of light
skin and "good hair", maybe big lips,
maybe a big bum, but hardly ever
on someone with darker skin.
When a black person says
they're only into white people
that's internalised racism.
When a white person says
they're only into black people
that's fetishisation, which is also
a form of racism. If their skin
or racialised features matter more
to you than the person within,
that's racism. I can't be your friend
without calling this out. Your ignorance
may be innocent but the racism is real.
I want both of you to think about how
what you said might make me feel.'

Lennie takes a long toke on the spliff,
which he has been holding on to
the whole time he's been talking.
He holds his breath, then starts laughing,
smoke spluttering from his mouth
like a backfiring engine.

He passes the spliff to Sienna. 'I meant
what I said, I just didn't mean for it to come out
as angry as that.'

Two bouncers come over to us.
The bigger of the two points to Lennie
and me and says, 'You two need to leave.'

'Why, what have we done?' asks Lennie.
The smaller bouncer replies, 'You're making
a scene,' he sniffs, 'and you're smoking weed.'

Out of the corner of my eye, I see Sienna
edge away and put out the spliff under the toe
of her red stiletto. She goes back inside.

'Off you go then,' says the bigger bouncer,
'unless you want to do this the hard way?'

MICHAEL: We've been kicked out 😞
You gonna come meet us outside?

SIENNA: I've just bumped into some friends
So I'm gonna stay 😊

Lennie and I walk along the seafront.
The bars and clubs are in full swing
but we don't have a plan as to where
to go next. 'I still can't believe Sienna
didn't leave with us,' I say to Lennie,
who shrugs.

'Oh, well,' says Lennie, 'this can be
a lads' night out instead. We could
go to that gay club you told me about.
I can be your wing-man. Find you someone
new to help you forget about Jack.'

I reply, 'I'm not in the mood. Do you
mind if we just head back to campus?'

'Good idea,' says Lennie. 'I've got
more weed in my room. Do you wanna
come for a smoke?'

At that moment, two drunk white guys
in suits stumble into us. They're in their
twenties but don't look like students. One
of them asks me: 'Got any weed for sale, *bro*?'
He has crooked teeth and a patchy beard.

I'm not sure if he overhead what Lennie
was saying or if he just saw two black guys
with locs and jumped to conclusions.

I reply, 'No, mate.'

His suit is light grey with white shirt
and black tie. He turns to Lennie and
asks, 'How about you, *big man*?'

The second guy, who had been quiet
until now, gets in my face. 'You're a liar!
I can smell it. How much?' He is clean
shaven and his breath smells of beer.
His suit is navy blue with a white shirt
and red tie; he reaches into his blazer
and pulls out two twenties and a fiver.

Lennie pushes Blue Suit away from me.
'Back up, man. My friend told you no.'
Lennie stares him down. 'And I'm telling you
both to keep walking.'

Fight or flight?

Money still in his left hand, Blue Suit puts
his hands up in the air in surrender, says,
'Sorry,' first to Lennie, then to me: 'Sorry.'

Grey Suit stands tall, smoothes down
his black tie and buttons up his blazer.
'Put your money away, Colin. Let's go.'

As they walk away, I turn to Lennie
and say, 'On second thoughts, let's go back
to yours.'

Back on campus, after another spliff
with Lennie, I stumble to my room.

In my bathroom
I go right up close
to the mirror
as if to kiss
my reflection,
I pull back my hair
away from my face,
trace my left cheek
bone and jaw line,
run my left index finger
down my nose, then
pick up the scissors:
This is the change. I cut.

Letting loc after loc
drop to the floor.

I'm shedding
something other
people use to define
me, falling to my feet.

For a moment, I think
I see them slither
like Medusa's serpents.

I gather my hair from the floor
and hold up this fistful of me
that I don't want any more.
I look in the mirror and laugh
at what I see. Cutting it myself
felt fantastic but now
I need to get it finished professionally.

My poster of Bob Marley
has come unstuck
at the top right corner
and droops down over itself.

I smooth it up and push
the Blu-tacked corner back
onto the wall. 'Nothing's changed
between us,' I say to Mr Marley.

In the morning,
I go to the one black barber shop
in Brighton; it's like any black barber shop
you'd find in London. The barber by the door
has an empty chair, the others
are busy cutting hair. I ask him
if he can give me a trim and fade.
I think of Kieran from school and
how his fade always looked so fresh.

'No problem. Are you a student?' he asks.
'If so, you get a student discount.'

'Yeah.'

He asks what I'm studying as he gestures
towards his chair.

'English,' I tell him as I sit down.
He puts the cutting gown over me
and fastens it at my neck.

He asks, 'What kind of job will you get?'

I tell him, 'I want to be a writer.
I write poems and one day
I want to publish my own book.'

He asks what I write about.

I don't say, *Coming out as gay*.
I don't say, *Sleeping with men*.
I say, 'Identity and stuff.'

He doesn't ask me anything else.

Mum and Anna
finally come to Brighton for a day trip.

We're walking along
the seafront and Mum says,
'We were going to
surprise you on your birthday
but you sounded so
stressed about your essays,
we decided that we
shouldn't disturb you.
We've missed you
so much. I can't believe
you cut your hair.
I'm so glad you told me
on the phone. It would
have been such a shock.
You don't look like
yourself any more.'

Anna scoffs. 'That's a silly
thing to say, Mummy.
If he is himself, how
could he not look like himself?'

Mum replies, 'Okay,
clever clogs. Maybe you should
be at university already.'

Anna laughs. 'I've not even done
my GCSEs yet, Mummy.'

'What I mean,' says Mum,
'is I used to cut your hair.
You look like you did
when you were a little boy.'

I turn to Anna.
'What do you think of it?'

'It looks good but
don't you miss your locs?'

'Not really. I feel lighter now.
People can't make assumptions
about me. Like, before I cut them,
I was here on the seafront, *right here*,
and this guy came up to me
asking if I could sell him some weed.
When I said no, he *actually* said,
"You're a liar!" Can you believe that?'

Anna replies, 'But
you don't know if that was
because of your hair;
it could just be because you're black
and he might think
all black men are drug dealers.
It was a white guy, right?'

'Yeah, he was
white but…' And I pause.

It hadn't occurred to me
until Anna said it just now:
the assumption
people make that I'm a drug dealer
might not be about
a hairstyle, it could just be
because I'm black.

We walk in silence for a while
but the seagulls
are still talking.

'You don't smoke weed,
do you, Michael?' asks Mum.

'No, Mummy. Not really.'

'What does "not really" mean?'

'It means I don't buy it
and I certainly don't sell it,
but if I'm offered by a friend,
I might have some.'

'You're here to study,
Michael, not to do drugs.'

After we've eaten,
we go to the arcade on the pier.

Anna and I
compete on the dance battle machine
and then the air hockey table.

Then the three of us
take a ride on the roller coaster
at the end of the pier:
Anna and me in a seat together,
and Mum behind.

I feel the chilling
sea breeze on my newly exposed
head and ears,
as we speed the winding tracks.
There's one point
where it feels like it's going to launch us
into the sky
and we might take flight for a second before
plummeting into
the water.

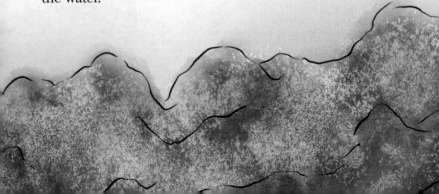

I imagine us all dying
like this, strapped
into our seats, unable to get free,
sinking together
in a roller coaster carriage.
It's just a momentary
thought but it feels so real.

I take a sharp intake of
cold air and grip Anna's hand.

To have a loving family
is to feel afraid and yet believe
you are going to be all right.

Mum and Anna
want to go shopping
in The Laines
and North Laine.
A bunch of quirky boutique shops.

Mum says if I come
she'll buy me something.
And this is always
how she gets me
to come shopping.

Once, when I was still
in school, Mum said to me,
'You're gay, you're meant
to like shopping.'

I didn't speak to her
for a week.

Two hours later,
Mum and Anna
have four shopping bags each.
I am wearing a new
black woolly hat,
and in my shopping bag
I have a pink shirt,
black trousers and shoes
that Mum picked for me.

I walk them back
to the train station,
where I met them
five hours earlier
and when I hug
Mum, she does
not let go – when I do,
or when I drop my arms
to my side, she squeezes
me tighter.

Anna says, 'Mummy, we're going
to miss the train.'

Mum mumbles
into my shoulder,
'I don't care.
There'll be another train.'

I realise Mum is crying.
I wrap my arms back around her.
I hadn't realised she missed me
so much.

When she finally lets go,
she says, 'Oh, I almost forgot.'
Mum reaches into her handbag
and pulls out the flamingo teddy.
'Why did you want me to bring this?'

'To remind me of home,' I say,
because I think it sounds right.

Really, it's gonna be part of my drag act.

When Drag Soc meet the following week,
it feels like a homecoming.
My drag family try to help me
develop my character more fully.

I've picked my lip sync song:
'Back to Black' by Amy Winehouse,
but the version sung by Beyoncé
on *The Great Gatsby* soundtrack.

I've brought my heels with me,
and Mzz B lends me a black feather boa.

I haven't decided on my dress yet,
so I rehearse my lip sync for them
in my regular attire – jeans and a jumper –
but with my high heels on my feet
and borrowed boa around my neck.

I feel a little closer to becoming.

A lip sync is a mime

to someone else's voice,
or even your own voice,
but it must be pre-recorded.

It could be a pop song;
a famous speech from a film,
a soap opera, a politician –
something familiar –
but your performance
should feel original.

You're not trying to be
that person, you're using
their words to say
something new.

David says he can lend me a black
tutu and leotard to wear for my drag.

Outside Drag Soc, David is Katy.
As we walk to her room on campus
to pick up these items of clothing, I ask,
'So, why do you have a tutu if you're
a drag king?'

'I just have a tutu,' she tells me.
'I just wear it sometimes for fun.'

Katy's drag king act is David Peckham.
Modelled after the footballer David Beckham?

'You do know who David Beckham is,'
says Katy. 'Victoria Beckham's husband.
I wear the kits for the different teams
he's played for but I do Spice Girls lip syncs.
I add a bit of facial hair.' She pauses.
'Are you gonna shave off your beard?'

'No, that would defeat the point,' I say.
'But what *is* the point?' she asks
bluntly – it doesn't feel offensive.

'You don't seem to want to change
much about yourself for the show,'
she says. 'You want to keep the beard
but still pretend to be Beyoncé?'

'That's not it,' I reply. 'I don't want to
pretend to be anyone, not any more.'

'So who *is* The Black Flamingo?'
asks Katy, with genuine curiosity.

———

I reply,

'He is me, who I have been,
who I am, who I hope to become.
Someone fabulous, wild and strong.
With or without a costume on.'

Katy's wardrobe is full of colour;
it reminds me of Camden Market.

I look down at my grey jumper
and navy jeans and think about
the rest of my wardrobe. This is
my uniform. I have left school,
but look at how I still conform.

The only bright thing I own is the
pink shirt that Mum bought me.

A pink faux fur coat catches my eye.
I ask, 'Can I borrow this as well?'

'Yeah, of course,' says Katy. 'There's
a matching handbag, if you want it.'

It's coming together, I think. *All I need
now is a wig and make-up.*

First, I do the easy part: I go into town
to the party shop and buy a pink wig.

It's the classic pink bob: the pinkest pink
and iconic bob style. It's a short bob
with a fringe, like the one Natalie Portman
wears in the strip club in the movie *Closer*,
like the one Scarlett Johansson wears
in the karaoke scene in *Lost in Translation*.

But I know when people see it on me,
they'll automatically think Nicki Minaj.

Next, to Debenhams
department store, to the make-up section.
No one else in Drag Soc has my complexion;
Mzz B is several shades
darker than me. So I know I need to buy
my own foundation. I'm not sure what else.

There are so many brands to pick from
but behind one of the counters
I see a person with a beard and a full face
of make-up. I approach them, smiling.

Their name badge says: 'Eden'.

I tell Eden about the show and how I want
to look. They give me a tutorial:
concealer, foundation, contouring,
highlighting, blusher, lip liner, lip colour,
mascara, glue-on lashes, eye shadow
and finally nail polish.

I notice two girls in school uniform watching.
They approach us.

'You look amazing!' one of them says to me.
'Can we take a picture?'

I feel elated!
Both of the schoolgirls take
a selfie with me and then together,
on either side of me.
When the girls go,
the tears begin.

Eden hands me a box of tissues.
I wipe my tears and see the black and brown
make-up on the crumpled white tissue
in my hand. I look in the mirror.
I don't feel fabulous any more.

My first time in a full face of make-up.
I feel self-conscious and overwhelmed.
I ask Eden to pass the make-up wipes,
which they do. Then Eden says,
'I get 50 per cent staff discount,
if you want to use it?'

Costume Confidence

I masquerade in make-up
and feathers, and hope to be applauded.
I evoke you as a metaphor;
attach my meaning to you.
Oh, Black Flamingo, here I stand
in your shadow. You are
my costume, my muse,
my poise and my strut,
my poetic and my purpose
but when I am naked
and plainly spoken
I don't feel so worthy of attention.

I have it all here,
laid out on my bed,
wig and make-up,
leotard and tutu,

tights and heels,
feathers, faux fur,
but I'm not ready
to put it all on yet,

I'm not sure what
I'm putting it on for,
I'm still not sure exactly
what I'm trying to say.

Drag Soc's show is tomorrow
and I've invited Mzz B round
to my flat to see my act in full.

I wanted to be ready before
they got here but I'm not
happy with my make-up,
I've put it on and taken it off
three times. I know it's not
the most important thing.

I imagined opening the door
looking perfect, in character
being shady and charming
and confident and fierce,
but right now I'm a wreck.

My desk is covered in make-up
and wipes with the brown,
black, pink, red, silver and gold
I've been trying to apply
to my face, and now I'm a mess.

When Mzz B arrives, I explain,
'I'm not ready. I can't do this.'

Mzz B slides
my make-up and wipes
to one side of my desk,
and perches on the space

they have cleared.

'Your lip sync is great,
your choreography is good,
and your poetry is wonderful!

Make-up isn't what makes your act.
Your passion and story are what
the audience really wants to see.

Believe me, honey, you are ready.
Look, I'll do your make-up myself,
if I have to.

Actually,
I won't have time for that.
But one of the others will.
We're a family.
We've got your back.'

They get up to leave.

'Before you go,' I say, nervously,
'I want to add something to my act.'
I go over to my bed and open my laptop.

'A PowerPoint presentation?' scoffs Mzz B.

'Kind of. It's some people I've found
online who I think are inspiring. Can I
show it to you, please?' I hand Mzz B
my laptop.

I watch them clicking through and nodding
in approval. 'This is pretty good, honey.
I mean, you're never gonna get everyone.
But this is a good start.'

'I was thinking I could add you to the list,
if you wouldn't mind?'

'*Me?!*' Mzz B says, exaggeratedly,
'Well, I don't see why not,' handing me
back my laptop with a big grin.

When Mzz B leaves, I'm feeling excited
and I decide to call Lennie to invite him
to the drag show.

Before I get the chance to speak,
Lennie says, 'You must be telepathic.
I was about to message you.
My cousin, Kim, is here from London
and she was telling us about a gay club
that plays hip-hop, R&B, dancehall
and Afrobeat. Kim said it's basically a black
gay club. She's going tonight and I
said Sienna and I would go along. Kim's driving
back to London. Do you wanna come?
It will be me, you, Sienna and Kim.'

'Please come, Mike!' says Sienna,
in the background.

'Since when have you been making plans
with Sienna?' I ask Lennie.

'Since you went AWOL,' Lennie replies.
He's right, I've not been a good friend lately.
I've been self-absorbed.

'Can I invite someone else?' I ask.

'Hold on,' says Lennie,
and the phone goes silent,
then, 'Yeah, Kim says there's space
for one more in the car.'

'They're in London already,' I reply.
'Remember I told you about my friend, Daisy?'

'Daisy? Oh, yeah. She has a girlfriend, right?'

'Yeah.'

'That's a shame, she sounded like
my cousin's type.'

I hear Sienna and another girl, who must be Kim,
laughing.

'I'll text you Kim's address and Daisy can
meet us there at...' Lennie pauses.

'Nine,' says Kim.

'Nine,' repeats Lennie. 'Come to mine ASAP.'

MICHAEL: I'm in London tonight!

DAISY: Yaaaay!!!! Will you be at your mum's?

MICHAEL: No. I'm going to a club with friends from uni. Wanna come?

DAISY: Which club? Where is it?

MICHAEL: I don't know. We're meeting at 9 at someone's flat. I'll send you the address

DAISY: But what kind of club? What music?

MICHAEL: Black gay. R&B hip-hop

DAISY: You know I can't dance to that! 😳

MICHAEL: Just come! It will be fun!

DAISY: Will you protect me from the lesbians?

MICHAEL: 😂 😂 💀

In the queue for the club, it's me,
Daisy, Sienna, Lennie and Lennie's cousin,
Kim. We had pre-drinks at Kim's flat
and everyone is getting on.

Looking down the queue, I realise
I'm a bit too smartly dressed for this place.
I'm wearing the pink shirt, black trousers
and black shoes that mum bought me.

Daisy is wearing a glittery red dress.

Earlier, I joked that it looked the same
as the dress she bought in Year 9.
'It *is* the same dress.' She laughed.
'I dug it out for old time's sake.'

Kim, who is softly spoken and petite,
is wearing an oversized black tracksuit
and fitted cap, and looks like a teenage boy.

Sienna asked her earlier if she's a trans man,
to which she replied, 'Nah, I'm a soft butch.'

Sienna is wearing her green dress
and Lennie is wearing his green tracksuit.

We get into the club and there's a lot
of people dressed like Kim. But
there are also people of all shapes and sizes
in tight, figure-hugging dresses
and short-shorts with crop-tops
showing off flat stomachs, abs
and bouncing bellies. *It's beautiful!*

Most of the people are black. Everyone
is dancing. It's not a song I recognise but
I feel the beat and nod my head to it.
'Let's get a round of drinks,' says Lennie.
'Good idea,' replies Sienna. 'To the bar!'
And we all move towards it together,
all except for Kim, who has disappeared.

I'm looking into the crowd for her when
I see him. But I must be imagining this.
Wishful thinking. It couldn't possibly be.

'Daisy, Daisy, look over there! You see
that person doing the headstand? Over
there? Behind them there's a person
with green hair. To the left of them. See?'

'*No!* It can't be!' says Daisy, gripping my
arm, as we stare into our recent past together.

'It looks like him, doesn't it?' I say. And
for a second I think he's looking back in our
direction.

'Yeah,' says Daisy, 'but even if it is, you
can't assume he's gay just because
he's here. He could just be here with
friends.' She points at Lennie and Sienna
kissing by the bar.

We're both watching him intently.
'Did he get hotter?' asks Daisy.

'No,' I reply. 'He looks exactly the same.
Maybe you're just less racist now?'

'Oh my god, Michael, you're such
a bitch. What's happened to you at uni?'

I don't know how to begin answering that.

I continue watching, as he says something
to the person with green hair,
then disappears in the crowd.

If Daisy hadn't seen him too,
I wouldn't have believed this.

'Mikey, here's your drink,' says Lennie,
handing me what I assume must be a rum
and Coke, carrying on from what we were
drinking at Kim's flat. 'Who are you two
checking out?'

'He's gone. We thought we saw a guy
we both went to school with. But I can't see
him now.'

My face must be showing all my emotion
because Lennie asks, 'Why don't you go
look for him? Where did you last see him?'

I think of school and him
waving at me from the football cage.

'It's too packed in here to find anyone.
We've already lost your cousin.'

Lennie laughs. 'Kim's not lost, she's
in there, exactly where she wants
to be, trust me. She's a ladies' man.
The stories she's told me. She's a player.
A real heartbreaker.'

I feel a hand on my shoulder. 'Excuse me,'
he says, close to my ear and I turn to him.
'Michael? You've cut your hair, but I recognised
you from all the way over there.'

Kieran is wearing a tight black top and I
can see the outline of his pecs and the top
of his abs. His jeans are black and tight,
his shoes are black boots, maybe suede.

'Kieran, yeah, hi. Remember Daisy?'
I'm nervous, I don't know what to say to him.

'Yeah, of course, you were always together.'

He opens his arms and hugs Daisy
and I'm jealous that she got to hug him first.

I blurt out without thinking, 'Can *I* get a hug?'

He smiles. 'I've got a better idea –
how about a dance?' He winks.
'Why not give this brother a chance?'

I hand Daisy my rum and Coke
and take Kieran's hand.

He leads me to the dance floor.
Beyoncé's 'Sweet Dreams' is playing now.

Dancing with Kieran is better than a dream.
He puts his hands on my waist
and pulls me towards him.
He bends both his legs to bring his groin
in line with mine
and we sway side to side,
finding a mutual rhythm.

His right hand leaves my waist
and then it's stroking the side of my face.
I lean my head into his hand.
I once saw him knock someone out
with this hand. He lifts my chin
and he leans in and kisses me,
so softly, no tongues. Just a peck.

Then he leans back and smiles.
Puts his right hand on my waist again.

Kieran from school.
Kieran who I watched playing football
in P.E. and at lunchtime.
Kieran who was kind to me,
always so kind. Was *this* the reason why?
Does it matter now?

'*Kieran!*' comes a voice from behind me.

'*Kieran!*' comes the voice again. Now
I see who it belongs to: the girl with green hair.
'Kieran, your sister is outside throwing up.
I'm ordering a taxi *now*.' Clicking her fingers
on the word 'now'.

His hands drop from my waist.
'Oh! Shit!' says Kieran. 'All right, I'm coming.
Just gimme a minute.'

'Okay, you have *literally* one minute.' And
she stands there with her arms crossed.

'Why don't you give me your number?'
I say, handing Kieran my phone. I can feel
the Death Stare of Miss Green Hair.

'Yeah. Cool,' says Kieran, as he types
his number into my phone. He hands it back.

Miss Green Hair claps her hands together
once on the word, '*Wonderful!*' as sarcastic
as she could be. 'Now, let's go, Kieran.'
She pulls him through the crowd. And I'm just
thinking: *Miss Green Hair is so fierce!*

I look to where my friends are by the bar.
None of them are looking in my direction.
So I head the opposite way to the toilet.
I lock myself in a cubical and write a poem
in my phone.

I Wanna Be Fierce

I've been friendly.
I've been frightened.
I've been fake.
But I've never been fierce.

I've been frustrated.
I've been forgotten.
I've been forgiving.
But I've never been fierce.

I wanna be fabulous.
I wanna be flamboyant.
I wanna flaunt what I've got.
I want to be fierce.

I go back to the group.

'I'm gonna go,' I say to whoever is listening.
Lennie looks at me sympathetically.
'Mikey, what happened with that guy?'

'It was nice,' I say, 'but he had to go.
And I'm not feeling this place any more.'

Sienna says, 'Well, we were just talking
about heading back to Kim's.'

As soon as we get in the taxi, I fall asleep
on Sienna's shoulder.

'Not all angels have white wings,'
says The Black Flamingo in my dream.

I am also a black flamingo
in this dream. The two of us are

standing on the pebbles
of Brighton Beach. The sea-foam

laps at our webbed feet.
Seagulls circle above.

'Who are you?'
I ask, taking one, two steps closer.

'Michael Brown,'
says The Black Flamingo, unmoved.

'Michael Angeli,'
I reply, spreading my wings.

'Mikey,'
says The Black Flamingo,
spreading his to match mine.

'Michalis,' I squawk.
'Mike,' he squawks back.

We peck at each other,
locking beaks once, twice.

The seagulls are laughing.

We back away slowly and fold
our wings.

I wake up.

Shit!

I'm meant to be on campus this morning
handing out flyers. It's Drag Soc's show tonight.
I leap up off the sofa, step over Lennie
and Sienna on the floor. Pat myself down:

Where's my phone?

Step back over the sleeping couple
and search between the sofa cushions.

Found it!

I run out of the door, to the Tube,
to get to London Victoria station
and on a train back to Brighton.

KATY: Do you still need help this morning?

KATY: Rise and shine!

KATY: On my way to help with your make-up

KATY: I'm outside

KATY: Where are you?

KATY: You dirty stop-out!

KATY: I've gone back to mine to get ready

KATY: See you at Library Square?

KATY: Are you okay?

KATY: Are you still coming today?

KATY: Let me know that you're all right

KATY: Mzz B is asking me where you are

KATY: ??

MICHAEL: Katy! Tell everyone I'm so sorry!

KATY: What happened?

MICHAEL: I went to London last night
But I'm on my way back now
I won't be in drag but I'll give out flyers

KATY: OK. I'll tell Mzz B you're on your way

MICHAEL: 🙏

MICHAEL: You awake? I'm on the train to uni

DAISY: Yeah. You okay? How was Kim's?

MICHAEL: I fell asleep in the taxi
Then I woke up there this morning

DAISY: We were all drunk

MICHAEL: Was Kieran really there?

DAISY: Yeah! Don't you remember?

MICHAEL: Kind of. But remind me?

DAISY: You danced. You kissed!!!!!

MICHAEL: You saw?

DAISY: Yeah! It was so cute!

MICHAEL: Do you think I should text him?

DAISY: Obviously

MICHAEL: What should I say?

DAISY: Just say, 'Hey, it's Michael'

MICHAEL: 👍

MICHAEL: Hey, it's Michael

The whole of Drag Soc is meant to be
in costume in front of the library.
Everyone is, but me. I'm two hours late.
Mzz B is more than disappointed when
they see me.

'Save your excuses. Just hand these out,'
they say, pushing the pile of flyers
into my chest. They shake their head
and turn away.

They go to the portable sound system
and pick up the microphone. 'Tonight,
Drag Soc presents Glitter Ball, the most
fabulous show you will ever experience.
These amazing drag kings and queens
will entertain and educate you in a way
that the books in this library could never do.'

Katy says,
'Don't worry, I understand how intimidating
doing drag for the first time in public can be.'

I tell Katy,
'Honestly, I was gonna do it
but I had the craziest night.
I met a guy who I
had the biggest crush on in school
but I never thought was gay.
He loved football and fighting
and, well, that was it, really.
I never thought he'd be into me.'

Katy says,
'Did I ever tell you about how much
of a controversy it was when David Beckham
wore a sarong, a skirt essentially, in 1998?'

I look at Katy, confused.
'I wasn't born then, neither were you.'

I look at her: England football kit,
fake stubble, hair in cane rows,
she really does look like the photos
I saw online of nineties David Beckham.

I think of Kieran.
Is he gonna message back?

I think of Justin Fashanu,
the first openly gay
professional footballer.

I think of how my sister
could wear my clothes
and play with my toys,
and it doesn't seem fair.

MICHAEL: Hey, it's Michael

MICHAEL: Hey, it's Michael

Mzz B comes over and says,
'There's always next term,
if you don't feel ready for tonight.'

'I am ready!' I exclaim.

Mzz B looks me up and down
and raises an eyebrow.

'I mean, I'm not ready right now
but I will be tonight.'

I see Simon and Mia
enter Library Square;
they don't notice me
at first and I'm relieved.

But I'm with a group
of drag performers
in their full costumes.

They see them
and me, the plain-clothed accomplice.

Mia is friendly in a way
that makes it clear she knows
what happened
between Jack and me.

Simon holds out his hand
for a handshake.
I place a flyer in his palm.

Mia says, taking the flyer
from Simon, 'OMG, yes!
I love drag!'

Simon plays it cool.
'Sure, we'll all come along,'

He says, 'Jack's here
for the weekend.'

I look behind them
and then behind me,
expecting to see
Jack.

'Relax,' says Simon.
'He's still asleep on my sofa.'

My palms feel sweaty,
I grip the flyers tighter, so as not to drop them.
I pause to compose myself.
'Sure. Feel free to bring him,
if you like.'

MICHAEL: Hey, it's Michael

KIERAN: Hey, Michael! You good?

I see Lennie and Sienna
enter Library Square,
they are hand in hand.

They come straight over to me.

'Well, look who it is,' says Sienna.

'I don't see anyone,' says Lennie.

'Oh, you're right. I thought I saw Mike
but he must have disappeared again.'

I roll my eyes. I think they rehearsed this.

'I'm sorry, guys. I had to get back here.
You were asleep.'

'You could've texted,' says Lennie. 'Kim
was calling you my rude friend who didn't say
goodbye or thank you.'

'Really?!' I feel mortified. 'Will you call Kim
so I can apologise?'

'I'm joking,' laughs Lennie.
'Kim was still asleep when we left.'

Relieved, I hit Lennie with my stack of flyers.

I explain about Drag Soc
and our performance tonight.
They both look surprised but
say they'll come along.

MICHAEL: Hey, it's Michael

KIERAN: Hey, Michael! You good?

MICHAEL: Yh. How's your sister?

KIERAN: Dee is fine. She just can't handle her drink

MICHAEL: I never knew you had a sister. How old is she?

KIERAN: What do you mean, you fool? You know my EVIL TWIN SISTER! You did a play together for Drama!

MICHAEL: WTF?! SHE'S YOUR TWIN?! How did I not know that?

KIERAN: I don't know, man

~~**MICHAEL:** Did you know she used to bully me?~~

KIERAN: I came to see the play. Not gonna lie, I was jealous when you kissed Rowan.

MICHAEL: I saw you at the cinema once. *Moonlight*. Do you remember?

KIERAN: Yeah, you were two rows in front of me. I was watching you more than the movie. You ran away when you saw me! 🏃🏾‍♂️😭

MICHAEL: 🙎🏻‍♀️ Were you on a date with that girl?

KIERAN: Were you on a date with Daisy?

MICHAEL: No. I'm gay

KIERAN: I was on a date. I'm bi

MICHAEL: ~~Are you single now?~~

KIERAN: Are you single?

MICHAEL: Yh 😊

KIERAN: Can I see you again sometime?

MICHAEL: Yh 😳

I'm happy about Kieran
but I can't help thinking
of Destiny
and how she bullied me,
not knowing
her own twin brother
would be the same kind of
sinner.

I think of her apology.

Did she only feel guilty
because it was something
so close to home?

I guess it doesn't matter.

I've already forgiven her,
and now Destiny's brother
could become my man.

GLITTER BALL

How to Do Drag

Your gender matters but should not
limit you. Know your audience; if possible,
see shows at the venue before
you perform there. Know that your audience
wants to be entertained. Know that
you don't necessarily have to give
your audience or anyone what they want.

Know that your audience makes
assumptions about you, your gender
presentation and the gender you were
assigned at birth. Your gender is not
what this is about. Remember that
this is a character, it's gender play
but not necessarily about your gender.

Know what you want to do before
you decide how you want to look.
Get friends to help you. If you don't
have friends, make some. Watch online
tutorials. Remember eyebrows are sisters,
not twins. Go to make-up counters in
department stores and try their products.

Keep the receipts – they often convince
you to buy more than you need
or will ever use.
Know that your skin tone
matters – not just for finding the right
shade of foundation but also for finding
the right tone for your act.
Do NOT do black face... unless...

No, just don't do it. Remember
make-up doesn't make your drag work,
clothes don't make your drag work –
your attitude and intentions are what
make it work. Aesthetic isn't everything
but don't look a mess... unless it's on purpose.
Do everything with purpose.

Be in control, even if you plan to
make it look like chaos. Read the room.
Be shady but not bitchy. Don't punch
or kick downwards at groups in society
with less power or privilege than you.
Tuck it away, if you want to. Stuff
your trousers with a sock, if you want to.

Wear a chest plate to give you pecs
and abs or boobs, if you want to. Pad
hips and bum, if you want to. Cinch
your waist, if you want to. Shave
or add hair, if you want to. Make none
of the above adjustments if you don't
want to.
Know why you want to do this.

If you don't know why,
why the hell are you doing this?
Really, why the hell are you doing this?
Ask yourself the night before,
Why the hell am I doing this?
Ask yourself the morning of,
Why the hell am I doing this?

Ask yourself the whole day
leading up to your first performance,
Why the hell am I doing this?
Ask yourself the evening of,
Why the hell am I doing this?
If you don't come up with an answer,
what's the worst that could happen?

A wardrobe malfunction? A tech disaster
with your music or lighting cues?
(Who do you think you are having music
and lighting cues?) You could fall off the stage.
You could literally piss or shit yourself
if you can't get out of your costume
quickly enough when you need the toilet.

When it's time to go on stage,
know that you're not ready but
this is not about being ready,
it's not even about being fierce
or fearless, it's about being free.

I don't have a clue what I'm doing
but that's not gonna stop me.

What It's Like to be a Black Drag Artist (for those of you who aren't)

It's knowing when you step on stage,
people will expect you to represent
all black people. It's being the only
black performer on the line up, one
of the only black faces in the room.

It's worrying if a white performer will do
a black face act. It's worrying your act
is too black, not universal enough. It's
worrying you're not entertaining enough
or fierce enough or shady enough.

It's giving up worrying about being universal
and being you. It's doing what feels true.
It's knowing that doing drag and being trans
are not the same. It's gender nonconforming.
It's gender bending. It's gender ascending.

It's a performance. It's not letting anyone
else tell you what your drag means. It's not
really for the audience. It's for your liberation.
It's knowing that after this nothing will be
the same for you. It's a rebirth.

It's giving birth to yourself. It's giving
yourself a new name. It's giving yourself
a new narrative. It's not letting anyone
forget your name. It's Marsha P. Johnson
smiling down on you. It's an ancestry.

It's a black queen who threw a brick
that built a movement. It's building
yourself up from zero expectations.
It's reviving your history. It's surviving
the present. It's devising the future.

It's afro futurism. It's afro centric. It's black,
black, blackity-black. It's batty bwoy, sissy.
It's queer, gay and faggy. It's yours
and it's yours. It's mine. It's time to step
out of the shadows and into the spotlight.

I'm finishing my make-up
in the dressing room, everyone else is ready.

I've done my whole face
but I'm struggling with
gluing on my eyelashes.

Mzz B says, 'Why didn't you do them earlier?
You should always start with the eyes.'

I snap at them, 'That's easy for you
to say but you never actually taught us
about make-up. You said the make-up
doesn't make our act.'

'Sure, honey,' says Mzz B,
'but any YouTube tutorial will tell you,
"You always start with the eyes."
That's just the basics.'

'Well, I don't *know* the basics!'
I scream. 'You were supposed
to teach us *the basics*, weren't you?'

'She needs to calm down,'
Mzz B says, turning her back on me.
'Someone give her a hand.'

And I like being referred to
as 'her' but I don't know why.

Katy helps me glue on my lashes
and re-apply the eye shadow
I smudged in my previous failed attempts
of lash adhesion.

'You look gorgeous, Mike,' says Katy.

'You look pretty handsome,' I say to her.

I look at everyone in their costumes
and it's like we're about to do a play
that we've been rehearsing for, separately,
our whole lives.

I've not seen anyone else's act in full
and they've not seen mine, either,
and yet we're about to do this show, together.

Mzz B introduces me
and the audience applauds lightly.

I recognise Sienna's solitary, 'Whoop!'
as I breathe deeply, off-stage
in the wings. I see Sienna
and Lennie sitting at the front

as I enter in by my borrowed pink
fluffy coat and handbag.
Pink wig and black heels,
the rest hidden for now.

I stand centre stage
in the spotlight and say,

'Put on that costume.
Wear what you want.
Where do you think
you're going dressed like that?

It doesn't matter
which costume.
A witch costume.
Werewolf. Vampire.
Zombie. Mummy.
Daddy?

"Where is love?"
Wear his love.
Despair is love
for what isn't
here any more,
or never was.

Love is a costume.

Son is a costume
you shrug on and off.

Mum is a costume
she squeezed
herself into, for you.

Dad is a costume
discarded
for other men
to try on.

Maybe it will fit
someone.
Maybe you
might grow into it.

Maybe it might shrink
to fit you, Barbie Boy.'

I decide not to pause for an applause
and I continue, 'As a young flamingo
I was given pink toys.'

I reach into my bag and
pull out the pink flamingo teddy
Mum bought in Cyprus.

'My family loved me,
my colour and flamboyance.
My difference was noted, not degraded.
It still made me feel separate.'

I deliver this next part directly to the teddy.
'The Black Flamingo looks in the mirror
of the salt lake's surface and doesn't
understand why a shadow stares back
at him. He doesn't look like the other
flamingos around him, he feels foreign
to his own flock, within his own family.'
I put the flamingo teddy back in the bag.

'You look amazing, Mike!' shouts Mia,
and I spot where she, Simon and Jack are.

'I know,' I reply, and the audience laughs.

'I always saw black excellence around me
and online but it didn't feel like it was mine
because I was not perceived as fully black.
I felt queerness made me even less black.

Being both black and queer,
affirming that I exist,
I am here and I have been here
long before this moment,
the first people were black
and queerness predates its modern meaning.
Queerness predates its derogatory meaning.
Queerness predates colonialism
and Christianity.
Queerness predates any hate attached to it.

I call myself black.
I call myself queer.
I call myself beautiful.
I call myself eternal.
I call myself iconic.
I call myself futuristic.

And you' – I point to Jack – *'can call me later.'*

I get a massive laugh from the audience.
Jack folds his arms, shrinking in his seat.

I spread my arms
in a gesture to the whole audience:
'You can call me
The Black Flamingo.

I'm going to give you some advice.
I'm going to tell you five things not to say
when chatting up a black flamingo:

Number one: "Can I touch your feathers?"
Number two: "Is it true what they say about
the size of your wings?"'

The audience laughs again, even louder
this time. I continue, feeling emboldened.

'Number three: "I usually prefer pink but..."

Number four: "I really love the contrast
between us."

Number five: "You know what they say,
once you go black you never go back."'

Lennie yells, 'Tell them!'

Next comes my
burlesque routine.
I perform a strip tease
with my lip sync
to 'Back to Black'
sung by Beyoncé.

I suggestively
open and close
the pink faux fur coat
before I let it drop
to the floor.

I snatch off
the pink wig
and throw it
into the audience.

I shimmy
with the feather boa,
then wrap it around
a smiling stranger in the front row.

I slip out of the tutu
and kick it away.
The crowd
go wild for it. For me!

I stand triumphant
in a leotard and heels,
a full face of make-up
and a beard
and say my final piece:

'I give thanks to
Adam Lowe, Ajamu X,
Alice Walker, Alicia Garza,
Alvin Ailey, Angela Davis,
Audre Lorde, Bayard Rustin,
Bessie Smith, Big Freedia,
Billie Holiday, Campbell X,
Carl Phillips, Chardine Taylor Stone,
Danez Smith, Dionne Brand,
Diriye Osman, Don Shirley,
Dorothea Smartt, Essex Hemphill,
Frank Ocean, Gina Yashere,
Jackie Kay, Jacob V Joyce,
Jacqueline Woodson, James Baldwin,
Janelle Monáe, Janet Mock,
Jay Bernard, Jean-Michel Basquiat,
Jericho Brown, Josephine Baker,
June Jordan, Kayza Rose,
Kei Miller, Keith Jarrett,
Kele Okereke, KUCHENGA,
Labi Siffre, Lady Phyll,
Langston Hughes, Lasana Shabazz,
Laverne Cox, Le Gateau Chocolat,

Lorraine Hansberry, Ma Rainey,
Marsha P. Johnson, Meshell Ndegeocello,
Mia McKenzie, MNEK,
Munroe Bergdorf, Mykki Blanco,
Mzz Kimberley, Nikki Giovanni,
Octavia E. Butler, Opal Tometi,
Patrik-Ian Polk, Patrisse Cullors,
Paula Varjack, Rhys Hollis,
Rikki Beadle-Blair, Roxane Gay,
RuPaul, Rudy Loewe,
Saeed Jones, Samira Wiley,
Sapphire, Skin,
Staceyann Chin, Stephen K. Amos,
Syd, Tarell Alvin McCraney,
Thomas Glave, Topher Campbell,
Tracy Chapman, Travis Alabanza,
Wanda Sykes, Yrsa Daley-Ward
and of course our very own,
"Em-zed-zed, you can call me Mzz B!"
Your art and activism has inspired me
to stand on this stage and feel free.'

Faces appear one by one
on the screen behind me,
all the people I mentioned.

I gesture towards them

and exit, into the wings.

There is a pause
before the applause begins.

Sienna's whooping is joined
by many more voices

and there's a huge cheer, as Mzz B
comes on, their photo projected behind them,
to announce the interval.

I go into the audience
to greet my friends. Sienna and Lennie
say, 'Well done!' in unison.

Simon, Mia and Jack come over,
so I introduce everyone. In heels
I can look Jack straight in the eye.
He asks, 'Can we talk privately?'

'Sure,' I say. I sashay towards
the smoking area, and he follows.
It's not so private but at least
we can hear each other here.
'So, what's up?' I ask casually.

'I've thought about you,' Jack says
in a hushed tone and steps closer,
'every day since that night together.
I need to tell you, I'm not straight
and you weren't the first guy
I've slept with. It's something I say –
I tell guys I'm not gay
to make them want me,
to become a trophy to be won,
it's a character I play;
it's my performance and I'm good at it.
Saying I'm straight suits me,
I wouldn't know how to be gay,
not publicly, not proudly,
not like you.
I couldn't do what you do,
I couldn't be so brave, so out there,
not where I live, where I work,
not in my family.
My brother knows
but doesn't want it to be true.
I'm sorry about what he said to you
and I'm sorry that I lied to you.'

I accept Jack's apology,
tell him I hope he figures out
his truth and how to tell it.
We hug and go back inside.

But that's not what happened,
that was just a sweet fantasy.

JUST BE A MAN

'Can we talk privately?'

'Sure,' I say. I sashay towards
the smoking area and he follows.
It's not so private but at least
we can hear each other here.
'So, what's up?' I ask casually.

'What's all this?' Jack points at me.
'My brother said you were
performing tonight but I thought
it would be poetry, like when
we first met. I didn't know
it was going to be a gay night
and you'd be dressed like a girl.
I just don't get this, Mike,
you're a talented writer,
you don't need to do all this,
it's just so embarrassingly extra.
Why can't you just be a man?'

And he's shouting at me now.
'Why do you have to hide
behind a costume like this?'

And I don't know if he's
talking to me or himself.

'You look ridiculous, Mike,
I'm embarrassed for you.'

And the whole smoking area
is looking at us and I don't know
if I should say what I truly
want to say to him right now.

Fight or flight?

I scream:
'You're embarrassed *for me*?
I don't need to be a *man*
for you or anyone else.
I don't perform for you
or anyone else.
What I wear is for me.
What I perform is for me.
What I write is for me.
I'm my own man
and you're a frightened
little boy. Who are you
to come here and shout at me?
We slept together once,
Jack. You don't know me.
You don't know my story
and I don't know yours,

but right now I don't want to.
If this is who you are, Jack,
I don't want to know you any more.

I was so excited to see you
here tonight to support me.
I thought we could be friends
or at least get some closure.
Well, *this* sure is *some closure*.
You know what? I'm embarrassed, too.
Embarrassed I lost my virginity
to you. What a waste. What a shame.
But you know what? Whatever!'

And this is most of our audience
in the smoking area. They saw
my performance earlier and *this*,
this is like an encore for them.

They all start to clap and cheer
even louder than before.

I turn and take a bow and when
I turn back there's no sign of Jack.

Removing my costume
in the dressing room,
I'm retelling the story
to my drag family.

I wish they'd been there,
but I know one of them
would have jumped to my defence
as soon as Jack started shouting.

I defended myself.
Maybe said more than I should
but I feel so good.
Even better than
I could have imagined.

I wish Jack had changed,
I wish he had apologised,
but I'm satisfied having
given him a piece of my mind.

I attempt to return
the borrowed items that
my costume is made of.

'Keep them,' says Katy.

'Even the coat?' I ask.

'Especially the coat.' She laughs.
'An ice cold queen like you,
you're gonna need to wrap up.'

Everyone cackles at this.

Katy continues, 'Merry Christmas!'

When I try to hand back
the boa to Mzz B, they say,
'It's yours. You were born
to wear those feathers!'

'Thank you,' I say, 'and I'm sorry
for shouting at you earlier.'

Mzz B says, 'I knew that anger
was nothing to do with me.'

EPILOGUE

How to Come Out as Gay

Don't.
Don't come out unless you want to.
Don't come out for anyone else's sake.
Don't come out because you think
society expects you to.
Come out for yourself.
Come out to yourself.
Shout, sing it.
Softly stutter.
Correct those who say they knew
before you did.
That's not how sexuality works,
it's yours to define.
Being effeminate doesn't make you gay.
Being sensitive doesn't make you gay.
Being gay makes you gay.
Be a bit gay, be very gay.
Be the glitter that shows up
in unexpected places.
Be Typing... on WhatsApp
but leave them waiting.
Throw a party for yourself
but don't invite anyone else.
Invite everyone to your party
but show up late or not at all.

If you're unhappy in the closet
but afraid of what's outside,
leave the door ajar and call out.
If you're happy in the closet
for the time being,
play dress up until
you find the right outfit.
Don't worry, it's okay
to say you're gay and later exchange it
for something else that suits you,
fits, feels better.
Watch movies that make it seem
a little less scary:
Beautiful Thing, Moonlight.
Be south-east London council estate,
a daytime dance floor,
his head resting on your shoulder.
Be South Beach, Miami,
night of water and fire,
your head resting on his shoulder.
Be the fabric of his shirt
the muscles in his shoulder, your shoulder.
Be the bricks, be the sand.
Be the river, be the ocean.
Remember your life is not a movie.
Accept you
will be coming out for your whole life.

Accept advice
from people and sources you trust.
If your mother warns you about HIV
within minutes of you coming out,
try to understand that she loves you
and is afraid.
If you come out at fifteen,
this is not a badge of honour,
it doesn't matter what age you come out.
Be a beautiful thing.
Be the moonlight, too.
Remember you have the right to be proud.
Remember you have the right to be you.

Acknowledgements

The writing of this book was made possible thanks to financial and in-kind support from The Authors' Foundation, Metal Southend, New Writing South, Seedbed Christian Community Trust, Spread The Word, Tri-Borough Libraries, University of Sussex Development and Alumni Relations Office, and University of Sussex Students' Union.

Thank you to my family, my friends, and my therapist.

Thank you to my mentors over the years, Benjamin Zephaniah, Charlie Dark, Jacob Sam-La Rose, Peter Kahn, and Polar Bear aka Steven Camden.

Thank you to Michael Twaits, and my graduating class of The Art of Drag course; Ben Connors, and Tate London Schools and Teachers for believing in this work at an early stage.

Thank you to my agent Becky Thomas for championing my manuscript and finding it a home at Hodder Children's Books; my editor Polly Lyall Grant for having the vision to see what was a collection of poems could be transformed into a verse novel; Anshika Khullar for their stunning illustrations; Alice Duggan for her amazing design; and the rest of the dream team that have worked on this book, including

Emily Thomas, Felicity Highet, Joelyn Esdelle, Katherine Fox, and Susie Palfrey.

Thank you to John Agard and Patrice Lawrence for advice and support when stepping into the world of writing for children and young adults; Elizabeth Acevedo, Jacqueline Woodson, Jason Reynolds, Sally Green and Sarah Crossan, whose books showed me how to do this; Year 10 students at Shoeburyness High School for being such an amazing early audience; Leila Rasheed at Megaphone for the mentoring session at the halfway mark; Malika Booker for the tough love in the final stages; Amyra Leon, Andrew McMillan, Caroline Bird, Joel Kelly, Joshua Judson, Keith Jarrett, Kostya Tsolákis, Matt Beavers, Sabrina Mahfouz, S.K. Perry, Travis Alabanza, and all the members of Malika's Poetry Kitchen and Keats House Poets Forum for the feedback and encouragement.

A special thanks to R. A. Villanueva, who, when I first shared a poem called 'The Black Flamingo' at Keats House open mic, said, 'That's gotta be the title of your next book.'

Thank you to Tom, who has supported me throughout this journey, and helped me to believe that happy endings are possible.

For more information and support, Dean Atta recommends the following charities:

Switchboard

https://switchboard.lgbt/

The LGBT+ helpline – a place for calm words when you need them most

Stonewall

https://www.stonewall.org.uk/

– working to let all lesbian, gay, bi and trans people, in the UK and abroad, know they're not alone

AKT

https://www.akt.org.uk

– supporting LGBTQ+ young people experiencing homelessness or living in hostile environments

UK Black Pride

https://www.ukblackpride.org.uk

– Europe's largest celebration for LGBTQ people of African, Asian, Caribbean, Middle Eastern and Latin American descent

Gendered Intelligence

http://genderedintelligence.co.uk/

– working with the trans community and those who impact on trans lives

Educate and Celebrate

http://www.educateandcelebrate.org

– equipping communities with the knowledge, skills and confidence to embed gender, gender identity and sexual orientation into the fabric of organisations

Schools OUT UK

http://www.schools-out.org.uk

– working to make our schools safe and inclusive for everyone

Amnesty International UK

https://www.amnesty.org.uk

– working to protect people wherever justice, freedom, truth and dignity are denied

The Anne Frank Trust UK

https://annefrank.org.uk

– an education charity, that empowers young people with the knowledge, skills and confidence to challenge all forms of prejudice and discrimination